Hope's Path to Glory

Also by Jerdine Nolen

Calico Girl
Eliza's Freedom Road

Hope's Path to Glory

❋ THE STORY ❋
OF A FAMILY'S JOURNEY ON
THE OVERLAND TRAIL

JERDINE NOLEN

•

A PAULA WISEMAN BOOK
SIMON & SCHUSTER BOOKS FOR YOUNG READERS

•

NEW YORK   LONDON   TORONTO   SYDNEY   NEW DELHI

*The author gratefully acknowledges
the kind help and valuable knowledge of Nikia Parker,
Constituent Services coordinator, Osage Nation,
Pawhuska, Oklahoma*

SIMON & SCHUSTER BOOKS FOR YOUNG READERS
An imprint of Simon & Schuster Children's Publishing Division
1230 Avenue of the Americas, New York, New York 10020
This book is a work of fiction. Any references to historical events,
real people, or real places are used fictitiously. Other names, characters, places,
and events are products of the author's imagination, and any resemblance to
actual events or places or persons, living or dead, is entirely coincidental.
Text © 2023 by Jerdine Nolen
Jacket illustration © 2023 by Adekunle Adeleke
Jacket design by Chloë Foglia © 2023 by Simon & Schuster, Inc.
Interior illustration © 2023 by Tom Daly
All rights reserved, including the right of reproduction in whole or in part in any form.
SIMON & SCHUSTER BOOKS FOR YOUNG READERS
and related marks are trademarks of Simon & Schuster, Inc.
For information about special discounts for bulk purchases, please contact Simon &
Schuster Special Sales at 1-866-506-1949 or business@simonandschuster.com.
The Simon & Schuster Speakers Bureau can bring authors to your live event.
For more information or to book an event, contact the Simon & Schuster Speakers Bureau
at 1-866-248-3049 or visit our website at www.simonspeakers.com.
Interior design by Tom Daly
The text for this book was set in Apolline Std.
The illustrations for this book were rendered in Procreate.
Manufactured in the United States of America
1222 FFG
First Edition
2 4 6 8 10 9 7 5 3 1
CIP data for this book is available from the Library of Congress.
ISBN 9781665924719
ISBN 9781665924733 (ebook)

For Judy Newton, who is on her glorious path

CONTENTS

CHAPTER ONE

A Broken Home

August 25, 1848
Alexandria, Virginia

I am inside my twelfth year. I serve Mistress Elizabeth
Barnett. She calls me her lady's maid. She says she is
teaching me to care for her personal needs. She says
she elevates me above the rest by calling me "servant" because all my work and chores are directed
inside the home and are most dedicated to her.
Though I feel no comfort from this, I must do what I
can in the best ways that I can to learn all that I can
to please her. The work is daylong and throughout
the night if Mistress has need of me. Of late, my mistress has fitful, worry-filled nights of one thing and
then another. So much has happened in these past
few years.

One day, I will be in complete charge of Mistress's
garments, from making repairs to washing and
pressing them to assure she is always neat. I am to
do the same for myself to keep myself presentable.
In a day, there is always much to learn. For now,
most of her clothes are ready-made. I am learning to
sew. I will be required to make some of the things
she wears.

The clothes we wear show our station in life. My
daily attire is a printed cotton dress, long sleeves, and
a stiff white cotton apron. I have one dress for Sundays

if it is required of me to wear for special occasions. It is the deep-blue-colored cloth, indigo, of the same style as my everyday wear. This dress includes a white collar. I am to keep myself neat at all times. Momma helps me with my hair. I keep it arranged in two large plaits pinned to my head.

Because Poppa—Ezekiel—had the good favor of the first mister of this house and Mistress Barnett, Momma—Adelaide—was allowed to keep me with her after she birthed me. Mistress feels it her responsibility to name each of the babies born here on Belle Hills Farm. "Favor or not," Mistress says, "money paid for you makes you *my* property." Momma would not accept the name she gave to me. My mistress named me Clementine. But secretly to me, I am not that name. Momma gave me the name Hope.

"I give this name to you, my daughter, because your birth moved me past my own understanding of these hard places within this world. You are *my hope*."

When I hear Momma voice these words, "my hope," it fills me up with what she aims my name to mean inside me. It fills me up with a feeling that each new day that rises with the sun brings a promise of something better—at least, for all our sakes, I must hold to this.

One of my morning duties is to read the news of the day out loud to my mistress. It is hardly a chore as reading brings me much satisfaction and clarity in my mind. Mistress taught me to read and write alongside her very own three boys. Jason, the eldest, is more a man than a boy. In our younger days, he spoke as easily to me as he did one of his brothers. Now I must lower my eyes and refer to him as Mister Jason when I speak to him on things my mistress would want him to know. He is soon to be twenty. Edward is older than me by two years. Then there is the youngest, Paul, who is ten years of age. All along the way of learning to read, Mistress tells me, "Clementine, I would not say this to others, but you have a quick and hungry mind for the words you learn."

Mistress is right in this. I love the way words can come together to make pictures in my head or stir feelings inside my heart. Words have such a meaning and a power like no other thing on this earth. I realize now what Mistress has given me is a great and dangerous gift. This ability to read allows me to think beyond this life and thus cause ideas to form in my mind. Sometimes I am too filled up with words. I fear they will spill out of my mouth and overflow as the river does after a bad storm.

There are times I am frightened by the thoughts that live inside me. When this new Mister speaks his opinion loudly on the good of slavery, words form, coming to me, speaking silently of slavery's wrongs—the awfulness of slavery. Though Momma says from what she has seen, this life here on Belle Hills Farm is not the worst it could be. But who would choose this life for themselves, for their children? Mistress and her new mister would not think kindly on what thoughts I hold inside me. I must keep this river from flooding.

Understanding this, I see why here in Virginia it is unlawful for me to read. I could be severely punished for my ability. Before now, my reading duties were never spoken of outside this home. But here, of late, the winds flowing through Belle Hills Farm carry change in mighty, quick, and misery-filled ways.

Even so, this gift and ability makes me feel proud inside myself. I see its worth. It helps me make sense of the world. It also gives me worry. I see that it sets me apart—different from all the others who work to serve here. We who work here are called "slave"—a word I do not like to hear or to speak. It has a most odd sound when I hear it spoken. It means a law says I am not first a human being or can belong to myself. It means I am property no different than this house the mister and mistress own, to do with as they please. It means my whole self belongs to someone else. This is something that is hard for me to understand. How can someone take possession of a person? Is not all of what a person is their thoughts, their mind—their heart? Momma says, "Be what it may, they can say what they think, but the true self lives inside the soul of every human person and no one on earth can touch it or take it from you."

Momma is wise. In truth, and above all else, we who are called this are *not* property. We *are* human persons. We are beings who are human too.

I am not alone in my desire for freedom, full citizenship, and equality. There is a man who comes from the nearby state of Maryland, Mister Frederick Douglass. Daily there is something of note in Mistress's newspapers about him. On his own, he taught himself to read. In the last two years, through his own efforts, he purchased his freedom. He speaks and writes on the ending of slavery.

Then there was a young woman such as me but born even before this country was founded. She too was an enslaved servant educated by the family she served. Miss Phillis Wheatley. She could read and write! My mistress tells me she wrote many poems on religion and criticized slavery. I am astonished that at thirteen years of age—which is my age plus one year—she *published* a poem! Then, a whole book of her poetry was published. Later in her life, the family she served did grant her freedom.

During the Revolutionary War, as this country was fighting for its independence, Miss Phillis Wheatley wrote a letter to General George Washington. In her letter she shared her hopes that he would apply the principles of freedom to all people in the new nation he was helping to build. General Washington was a very important man. He did many things to establish the United States of America. He became the first president of these United States. Though little has changed since Mistress Wheatley lived, her life inspires me. Her letter did not change Mister Washington's mind to end slavery.

Mistress gave me a copy of Miss Phillis Wheatley's book, *Poems on Various Subjects, Religious and Moral.* Inside this book, to make it mine, Mistress wrote, "For Clementine."

I was so happy with such a gift upon a gift—a book.

"It is the one thing I treasure more than I can explain," I told Mistress. But that night, when I was alone, I thought of my dear mother, and I see why she would give me such a name. Then I turned to the very last page of the book and wrote something to myself. I wrote: "For Momma's Hope." That night I had a most wonderful dream. It felt as if I was flying over a vast and strangely beautiful place.

In these days now, life here has changed a great deal and is changing ever more. This fact and a growing number of things have caused terrible quarrels and strife in this once-peaceful household since there is a new owner, Mister Uncle Howard Barnett.

Momma says, "Whether little or much—there is *nothing* we inside or outside this house can do to mend what is broken here."

There are upward of thirty of us who are bound to serve the lives of the mister and mistress and this home and farm. Joseph, who is in charge of the fields and the workers, said to Mister Uncle, "As we always did, in the earlier days, we need to keep rotating the crops to make a greater yield."

But these words Joseph said to this new owner caused such anger and fury to blow up as bad as a hurricane. This new owner, who was a banker before he became a farmer, feels he knows best. Yet this thriving farm is now failing. Each season with every poor yield, his anger grows, causing him to make damaging decisions and terrible threats.

He tells Mistress, "They are lazy and are not working hard enough in the fields. If things do not improve, we will have to sell one or two of them." My greatest fear is he means me. I have heard him say to Mistress that "Clementine could fetch a smart amount because of what she has learned in being a lady's maid."

Thinking on his words makes it hard for me to breathe. Momma says I must train my mind and my thoughts not to wander. But I am not so sure how I can do this. From my own reading of the newspapers and hearing Mistress read so many wonderful tales, I find my mind is filled with words. Sometimes at night to help me to sleep I let words I have read wash over me and pour through me like a waterfall.

Momma is the main cook and caretaker of the kitchen garden. I am her helper with the preparation of the meals when I am needed. Selby cares for the household cleaning and we three altogether keep up the washing of the clothing and linens. Poppa also serves in the dining room and cares for the wagons and horses. The old owner had pride in Poppa's attention to his horses and wagons and tending the wheels.

We each have many jobs to keep this household and family running. The rest tend cows, pigs, chickens, and the fields in planting and harvesting tobacco, wheat, and corn.

Momma says *this* new mister and our mistress should feel some happiness that the health of all is good in spite of the heat and miserable weather. Bad weather and workings of the farm usually coincide with normal happenings. But nothing is normal or usual here in these times.

Much of these days Mistress pines so. She does not flit and flutter happily around the house as she did before all these dreadful things happened in a row.

Quietly and often she squeezes my hand and whispers to me, "My heart is broken clean in two. This house is broken as well."

But Momma says the cause of these breaks happened long before these new things of late. The first awful break was three years ago, when the rightful mister of this house, Clinton Barnett, was drowned in the raging sea. For so long Mistress grieved. Momma says her grieving has never stopped. Nothing has come to still her deep hurt. The love between them was true. He, like the mistress, was usually more kind to us than some others.

Momma says the second break was so much worse than the first. Mistress married again two and one-half years ago. Her new husband, Mister Howard Barnett, is the brother of the deceased, was brother-in-law to Mistress, and is uncle to these three boys. He is the one who pronounced it proper for Mistress to marry because of his family line and interest in this plantation farm as well as we who serve it.

Some say happiness such as this cannot come so fast, so soon after death. In this, Jason is much like his mother. This union did not cure the sadness that sits deep like a well inside his heart.

Now has come the third and I fear final break. In this month of August, news has arrived, all the way from the west, of the discovery of gold found in the

American River at the base of the Sierra Nevada Mountains in California. Pure gold! Daily there are stories in the newspapers that people are becoming gold rich. It is said that gold fever has taken over the world.

They are saying there are chunks of gold pieces lying on the ground for the taking just as hogs would pick ground nuts. This gold fever has infected everyone. Mister Uncle has all the way disrupted this home with his ambitious thoughts and talk of mining for gold himself! From early in the morning until late at night he talks of nothing else—traveling to California to strike it gold rich. His talk is most unsettling to Mistress and the household.

Everywhere my mistress reads, and she reads so much in books, newspapers, and periodicals, are thoughts of gold. There are stories, opinions, and letters written by people who speak of their luck. She says the world has sure but lost its own mind with it. She has included our own president of these United States, James K. Polk. He encourages the people to advance to the west. He has often stated his belief that the United States is fated to expand across the continent, "stretching from sea to shining sea," to extend the boundaries of the country.

Yesterday morning, Mister Uncle spoke to Mistress about his plans to travel to California. He mentions often one John O'Sullivan, a journalist who refers to this westward expansion idea as "manifest destiny." Mister Uncle says traveling to California allows him to "manifest his destiny."

Last evening at dinner, Mister Uncle talked on and on without stopping of his plans to journey forth to help to manifest his destiny in the California gold fields. Finally, Mistress had enough. She spoke to her mister in a voice I had never heard her utter before. She made a most compelling argument to him.

"Stop speaking of this idea ... making such a journey. Do you know how much it frightens me if *you* should embark on such an expedition? It fills me with fear at the thought of losing another husband—to death— for a second time. It is something I could not bear."

"Then"—he turned to her quickly—"we must *do something*. We must find more expedient ways to raise money. If not, we must start selling *them*."

These words fill me with dread. I know Mister Uncle does not favor we who work here inside this home. On many occasions he states his dislike that we already have too many freedoms. I feel his anger often. I know it is because of my gift. I have heard him say things to Mistress about me that are troubling to him.

"Knowing how to read has given her an alertness. I do not like that it is there."

He knows it is a gift that I cannot give back. There are times I wish I could leave here to seek my fortune of a better life as it is described in the newspapers—manifest my destiny.

Daily are stories and published letters of those who have originally come from as far away as Europe, England, and Hawaii, emigrants who have come to these United States and traveled on to California to seek their fortune in gold. If I could speak truth, this talk of travel gives me much excitement and it thrills me. Mistress has me reading these sections of the paper first before I read any of the other news of the day. These adventure stories are most compelling.

Today, I wish I did not have this chore. Normally, this time of year is full of happy thoughts for the coming holidays. This day, December 9, 1847, is a day I will always remember. I am reading from the *California Star* newspaper, a story called "Distressing News." The story is dated February 13, 1847. I do not know how Mistress came upon these newspapers.

The story was written of two families of travelers, the Donner-Reed Party, who traveled by wagon train on the Overland Trail to California. They began the journey April 12, 1846, with eighty-nine emigrants in their group. Following a travel guide created by Lansford Hastings, the group was met with many misfortunes. They started the journey west much too late for the route they took. Hastings advised them to take an alternate road off the often-traveled Oregon and California Trail—expecting to shorten the journey. Later it was determined they added eighteen extra days and more than two hundred miles.

The unfortunate group reached the Sierra Nevada Mountains with their livestock and supplies in November. A terrible early snowstorm trapped them in the mountains for the four long winter months with no way of escape. The emigrants ate all the livestock they had. Without food, many people died from cold and starvation. Those who remained had to take horrible, unthinkable measures to provide food—using the dead for meat. A search party was put together to finally reach the survivors. Only forty-five of the eighty-nine who started reached California to tell the horribly sad story.

I do not want to read this to Mistress, but she compels me to tell her every sickening detail that befell the poor families. I know full well she already read it for herself. After I close the paper, she says, "Clementine, I forbid you to speak one word of what you have read to anyone."

I only wonder, how can I not? It is hard sometimes to stop the waterfall of words that come to me. Suddenly, I feel so weary in my heart and my head is heavy. Without asking "May I?" I lie down on the floor beside Mistress's bed as I did when I was much younger, when she would read stories to her boys and me. But these are not good-feeling thoughts I have. This is not a faraway fantasy of some distant land. This is a story of horror and truth. Now I feel I have caught whatever awful complaint that ails her.

While I lie here, after reading about these poor families, I wonder if I should have regret or hard feelings about this ability I have. It is a mighty, two-sided thing, like a sharp knife. I think to myself, there are many dreadful things in the world. We know this, including this station my family and I have in this life, and those like me who cannot do as others and manifest our destiny. First, this gift I have is a joy. It is also a responsibility. Each time I read, I am discovering something I never knew before. I learn of the hard places and happenings in the world—things I could otherwise never imagine on my own. These times I hold my little volume of Miss Wheatley's poems close to my heart.

Yet poor Mistress's sadness continues with now the third thing to break her heart.

Now the oldest son, Jason, is often speaking, first jokingly and getting more serious by the day, that perhaps *he* should be the one to take this journey west to the gold fields. Since the loss of her dear *beloved* husband, she worries more for him and fears for him—to lose him. He is much like his father in this way, unafraid and adventurous.

He has taken great interest in reading these news stories of traveling on the Overland Trail to find gold. Today, he nearly tears my ears off with such loud bursts of excitement.

"You see, Mother?" He runs to his mother's room. "Today in the paper I learn I am no different from many other twenty-year-old men. They, too, are embarking on this journey. See here, written in black-and-white," he says, pointing to the words on the paper.

"Here, Mother, those who plan to go west to seek gold are referred to as 'argonauts.' *Argonauts*, Mother! Just as in the story you read to me and the games of pretend that I played and longed for. Don't you remember? You read the story of 'Jason and the Golden Fleece' to me over and over again," he says, looking to me as though I should help her to remember.

"Mother, it is an excitement I cannot contain. It is my fate, Mother. It is my manifest destiny!" Then his voice softens.

"Besides, for once, Uncle is right. The crop yields are worsening. We badly need money to help this farm survive. I am only trying to maintain our father's legacy. If *he* were here . . ." his voice trails off. Then he starts again. "Mother. Please try to understand."

Poor Jason, I think. He cannot see how Mistress's pain and suffering grows bigger by each word with his excitement over such a journey. I, too, read that story. The word "argonauts" was used for those who traveled to California by sea from the East Coast of the United States to the west and the gold mines. He dares not mention this fact to Mistress to help plead his case. Traveling by boat is what sealed his poor beloved father's fate. He knows my mistress could not even consider an adventure journey, especially if it is to be over unknown and dangerous waters.

Momma and I have decided to explore. We discovered California on a map in the great library room. It is all the way on the other side of this country. "How in the world can anyone travel across all that land to reach gold in California?" she whispers, shaking her head.

After reaching California, there is no place else to go except into the waters of the Pacific Ocean. "It certainly will be a journey to the end of this world," Momma continues. Later, Momma quietly whispers to me, "This is Mistress's own fault for filling Jason's head with such tales."

This is true. Mistress admits it herself. Mistress is from the northern country of Canada. Before marriage and children, she was a teacher. She is a devoted reader who reads all the time. Daily she would read to us, her own children and me. There was a favorite, a myth, a very old story she read again and again. It was "Jason and the Golden Fleece."

It is the story of so long ago in a foreign land where a king and queen ruled and the kingdom prospered. The queen had given birth to a son, Jason. The people loved their king. The king's brother was jealous. He killed his brother and the queen. To save the infant, a wise man sent Jason to a faraway place for safety. The baby, Jason, grew into a fine young man. He was the rightful heir to the throne. He was fit to be king. When he returned to his homeland, he saw that his uncle, the king, was not a good leader. The kingdom had become very poor. The people were hungry and suffering.

Jason wanted to help. There were stories of a far-off land that was filled with riches and gold. In that place was said to be a sheep's wool or fleece made of pure gold that had magical powers. His uncle, the king, challenged Jason. He told Jason to search for the fleece of gold and if he could find it, he would be worthy to be king. The young man set off on the perilous journey across the dangerous sea to claim the riches the golden fleece was said to offer.

As a boy, Mister Jason never grew tired of hearing this tale.

The next morning Mister Jason follows Poppa around like a shadow all the while he does his work. Even without his mother's best wishes or consent, Mister Jason is making a purchase list of supplies such as revolving pistols, rifle, Bowie knives, belt hatchets, axe, superior wax taper matches in round wooden boxes, maps of California, and a money belt that is to be made to hold his gold. Mistress thinks he is too young to undertake such a dangerous journey alone. Momma thinks it would be wise for Mistress to let Jason take the journey.

Mistress herself goes to the barnyard where Poppa is tending the horses. I am to follow her. She turns to my poppa. "If he is to make this journey overland, you must go with him, Ezekiel. You have known him. You know his temperament. You have watched him being raised. You know his father would want you to do this. He will need guidance and help to keep him from the terrors of the world and unsafe roads.

"Help him to manifest this destiny he feels he must. Help him, Ezekiel."

I listen to her words and watch my poppa's face. I feel what he must feel. At once there is excitement of an adventure journey, but there will be no destiny for Poppa to manifest.

CHAPTER TWO

Traveling to the End of the World

January 2, 1849
Belle Hills Farm

The Christmas season seemed busier than ever,
though it was hardly as joyous. The house was much
more crowded than last year. Mistress's sister, Rachel,
had welcomed a new child into her family. Now there
were four young children. The young ones were not
aware of the unrest inside Belle Hills Farm. It made
their joy so much harder to bear.

Nothing felt the same. Everything felt strange and
new, inside me and inside this house. It was as if there
was not enough air to breathe. I did my best to stay
clear of Mister Uncle's regard of me. If I noticed him
gazing off in my direction, I would find some reason
to move from the spot he found me. Suddenly, the
walls of Belle Hills Home seemed too small to hold
all of the commotion growing inside me.

During the whole of days and the many festivities
Mister Jason made no more outbursts or mention of
his desire to travel west to find gold. There was an
uneasy quiet that created empty spaces inside each
room. I knew from hearing Momma and Poppa talk
he had already begun preparations for the journey.
He'd met often with Poppa, first to begin making lists
of supplies he would need, and then they left most
mornings at daybreak to return just before supper.

The day after Christmas, Mister Jason told Mistress he had business in Charles Town, in Jefferson County, Virginia. He and Poppa had already made several trips there. I suspect that is where they went all along. Whatever they were doing, and whomever they met, Poppa was quiet about everything to Momma and me.

"It is good we have the house back to ourselves," Mistress says this morning, the second day of the New Year. She, too, is happy to have the house empty of her relatives. The family said their good-byes at breakfast to travel home to Richmond, Virginia. In happier times Mistress and the boys would travel back with them to their home and return in early March with the milder weather. This year, she sent the two younger boys, Paul and Edward, to visit. She would travel later to retrieve them.

I am happy for the quiet and routine. Though this new year does not feel like others.

At dinner this night, Mister Uncle seems more out of sorts than usual. His anger fumes as we carry out the dinner rituals. Momma, Poppa, and I stand in our places around the room to serve the meal to the family. I feel fidgety as I await an order from Mistress or a family member to bring more food from the kitchen.

Mister Uncle drops his fork. I rush to retrieve it. Momma is quick to offer a clean one. As I kneel at his feet reaching for the fork, he speaks to me.

"Here," he says as I begin to stand again to return to my serving place. He hands me a small sheet of paper.

"Pass this on to your mistress."

I stumble, my legs almost giving out under me. I can see words on the paper: "Bill of Sale." Mister Uncle is beginning to make good on his promise to sell some of us to raise much-needed money. I gape at the other words on the paper. My heart pounds in my chest and into my ears. *Who* is being sold? My hand holding the paper begins to shake violently. My stomach churns. I steady myself placing my hand on the table as I hand the paper to my mistress, trying to hold back my sobs.

"It is a bill of sale," he announces. "You can read it yourself, can't you girl," he shouts. Then he looks to my mistress. "It is to transfer a family of slaves. I have decided to sell Ezekiel, Adelaide, and Clementine, from Alexandria, Virginia, to St. Louis, Missouri. There they are to serve my own cousin's family," he adds as he cuts his meat and puts the portion of it into his mouth. Hearing this news, I become too heavy for my legs, and I drop to the floor. Momma moves toward me. Jason, who is nearest, begins to rise. "Let her be," Mister Uncle sneers. I manage to stand on my own and use the wall to become steady.

"Think of this as a *gift*," he says, speaking in Poppa's direction. "At least I'm not separating you," he says, turning back to the food on his plate.

I look to Momma and Poppa to do my best to hold back my tears. Belle Hills is the only home I have ever known. I do not know why this new year has come to rip us all apart. I look to Mistress Elizabeth. She never glances up from her plate. She keeps her gaze down at her hands folded in her lap.

Then, Mister Jason clears his throat to speak.

"St. Louis?" Jason begins with a bright tone to his voice. "Why, my dear uncle, what a wonderful and unlikely coincidence. This is all very well and very good news! I am to be traveling there to St. Louis myself, *soon*," he says, and gives a nod in Poppa's direction. Then Poppa nods back as if the two need to agree that this was the proper time.

"There is a company, the Virginia California Mining Company, that is being formed in nearby Charles Town, Jefferson County, Virginia, just ten miles west of Harpers Ferry," Jason begins.

"The group is being formed by Mister Peter S. Cooper. He is to start the journey to California as of March third. I plan to travel with him and his company to the gold mines to seek my fortune. There are many men from nearby in these neighboring counties that have joined this party. I have been meeting with Mister Cooper since before Christmas holidays to procure passage with the VCMC. It is a process, Mother, to show myself worthy of the challenge of such an expedition. Every person must be fit enough to pull his own weight. Before I could join Mister Cooper's company, I had to pass certain physical tests in strength and in endurance—swimming, shooting—as well as references to my character. Mister Cooper knows the stamina required to undertake such an ordeal."

"What is the meaning of this?" Mister Uncle demands.

"Meaning?" Mister Jason says innocently. "I am explaining now, Uncle. I was introduced to Cooper by my friend Richard Evans Smith," Jason calmly continues.

"You know him, Mother. You and Father knew his family. They occupy Smith Hall Farm. When Father was alive, we sometimes would share family meals.

"Even as boys, Richard and I talked about some grand journey we would take together before we settled down with wives of our own to raise families. Since news of this El Dorado in California, we both see this is the time. For all of our lives, we have been discussing traveling together."

Mistress is sitting up, looking at and listening to Mister Jason as if she is meeting him for the first time.

"Now Richard has decided to take the eight-month journey to California by steamship around Cape Horn. Do not worry, Mother. I have decided to take the journey over land across the prairie to the gold fields. It is sure to be a wonderful and great adventure of a lifetime.

"The path to California begins on the well-traveled Oregon Trail. Independence, Missouri, near St. Louis, is where we start. Mister Cooper calls this the 'jumping-off point.' Isn't that clever? So, you see, Uncle? This *is* a coincidence.

"The journey is very well planned out. For now, the wagon trains will go around Fort Bridger, where the one trail becomes two. Those going to Oregon continue north while we, going to the gold fields, will veer south to California. However, Mister Cooper tells us new roads and better ways west are being discovered all the time.

"Somehow, Richard and I *will* meet up in California at the gold fields. I am sure to arrive well before he does as the trip on land takes five to six months. I'm told this route is just as wonderful, Mother— beautiful and wild."

We all are listening to Mister Jason as if he is telling us some wonder story from one of the many books in his mother's library. I cannot help but think Mister Jason's choosing to travel by land instead of water is a way of softening the blow of his plans.

"Mister Cooper refers to this jumping-off point of our journey as the 'Gateway to the West,' like those mountain men before him. Just as the explorers, Lewis and Clark before them."

Mistress seems a little relieved hearing this news but sits quietly for what seems a forever time. It surprises me that her breathing remains calm.

"Peter Cooper is a former army lieutenant. He is very knowledgeable about these trails. He has taken this journey six times and safely led other emigrants. He has many friends and acquaintances who call themselves mountain men and know these roads very well. Tomorrow, I plan to meet with him again to finalize matters. I will give him the initial five hundred dollars for the journey.

"In all, there are sixty-three men going. Five of the men in the group are traveling with their families. These men are mostly farmers and mechanics with two exceptions: a lawyer and a teacher. Everyone is seeking the freedom to live the life they choose and to better their lives, Mother. These are ever-changing times.

"We are all strong, able-bodied men who can endure such hardships. Some, like me, are going to the gold fields to seek fortune. Some are going for the adventure. Most speak of leaving these lives here. There are those who are taking their families—wives, children, and grandparents, as well as the family pet, for something new and better. Like many others before them, they are going west to create a new life—a *new way* of life, Mother—and riches beyond our dreams." He gives a hearty laugh.

Mister Uncle can say nothing.

"I will sign Peter Cooper's Memorandum of Agreement. I am using my own money and am of age to do so.

"The company has already voted Cooper captain of our wagon train west. He tells us the road is very well mapped and marked as thousands have traveled before. The US government has even established army posts and supply stations along the way. Though it may not be all the comforts of home, Mother, Captain Cooper assures us the road is hard but quite doable for young men such as myself.

"He gave me this overland guidebook showing a route over the trail that is useless. Now there are many more successful ways across the terrain." Jason removes a small book from inside his jacket and places it on the table.

"It was put out by Lansford Hastings; this is the guide used by the unfortunate Donner-Reed party." I hear these names and I shudder to remember the news story I read. Mistress shows no concern. She sits almost in admiration of her son as he continues.

"We will only be using it for some of the way, not the supplies list. I have been studying parts of it, but Cooper says there is no way I could finish reading it before we start." Then he pauses. "Oh, the company is to depart for California March third, from Harpers Ferry." Mister Jason pauses and turns to Mister Uncle with an afterthought.

"For you, Uncle," Mister Jason says. "I have a second copy and will pass this one on to you as you may have time to read it." He motions to me to hand-carry the book to deliver to Mister Uncle's side of the table. I do, but I do not look up.

"Charles Town? So soon?" Mistress says quietly. "March third?"

"Yes, Mother. That is two months from now. There is much to do to prepare," he says, leaning forward.

"We must start our journey from Virginia early enough to be ready to move overland when the ground is dry. Until then, the road over the plains is muddy from the heavy and early spring rains. We must wait for the new grass to be growing again for the animals to graze. We must also be well supplied with feeding grain for the animals. The animals must be kept well and in good condition."

Mistress quietly lays her knife and fork on the table and picks up her napkin.

"Oh, please be happy for me, Mother. For us, Mother," he says as he gestures toward Poppa and Momma, who are standing on his side of the table, and me, standing at the other end.

"Do not worry. I am sure to be successful in my pursuit." But Mistress says nothing as Mister Jason rattles on.

"Isn't it wonderful? There will be so much to see. Mister Cooper says many who take this journey are said to 'see the elephant.'

"Seeing the elephant," Mister Jason repeats aloud, and chuckles as he sits back confidently in his seat with satisfaction. "It does not mean officially *seeing* a woolly mammoth or a *real* elephant, Mother. It is used as a way to describe the magnificence of the natural spectacles of this land—the landforms and features you see along the California Trail.

"Cooper says it is an expression that means many things—most amazing and surprising as an adventure journey could ever be—to see something to have never been seen before. I'm sure not as surprising as the monsters Jason encountered in his quest for *his* golden fleece."

Mister Jason chuckles as he speaks so quickly. It seems he hardly takes a breath between his words.

"We will make our way by riverboat—steamship to St. Louis and eventually to Independence,

Missouri, our jumping-off point for the journey west. After leaving St. Louis, it will all be wilderness, Mother, probably not as wild as when Mister Lewis and Mister Clark scouted the first route west to the Pacific Coast but rough country, just the same.

"In this vast landscape, we are sure to encounter people of the wilderness, Mother, and every manner of person from around this globe as all are seeking their fortunes.

"You see, *we* will be good company for each other," Mister Jason says, gesturing again toward Poppa, Momma, and me. "It will hardly be so different from being within these walls of Belle Hills."

Mister Uncle has been quiet this whole time. But I can see his anger is rising and he is becoming eager to speak as he thumbs the pages of the book that caused such a disaster.

"You keep saying *we*," Mister Uncle says, never looking up from the pages of the book.

"Why, yes, Uncle! Ezekiel, Adelaide, and, of course, Clementine will *have to* accompany me on my journey. Your sale will have to be postponed. And who knows, I may make such a huge fortune, we will not have to sell anyone at all."

Mister Uncle stiffens.

"Surely, Uncle, you will not deny me *servants* on my journey. Who will make repairs on the wagon?

Cook my meals? Clean and mend my clothes? And if need be, if I am not as successful as I plan to be, on the way home to Virginia, I will see to it they are delivered to our cousins as promised."

"Then, it *is* settled," Mistress finally says on a long sigh and stands. "Ezekiel, Adelaide, and Clementine *will* accompany Jason on this journey."

I gasp. My eyes open wide. This time I do not drop to the floor. I steady myself against the wall.

"I see this as the only way," she adds.

Then she turns to Mister Uncle. "It is all good and well. You have helped provide the solution assuring Jason's safe passage!"

She turns to Poppa and addresses her comments to him.

"And I expect you to remember your responsibility to this family and accompany Jason on this quest." I hold tight to my little volume in my pocket, wondering how this can be. How can life change so suddenly?

Mister Uncle clenches his fist and pounds the table.

Mistress, seeming very relieved, says, "On the issue of raising funds for our farm, I will sell a piece of jewelry I hardly wear anymore." She stops and looks around the room at each of us. "I think, then, it is settled."

Settled. The word repeats itself in my mind. All the while Mister Jason spoke, the room around me swirled and seemed to dissolve. It is difficult to hold myself up. I am grateful for the solid wall.

Sold? I am to be *sold*? I am sold away from my home. I know of no other place or how to live anywhere else. A journey? I am taking a journey across a wilderness of unknown dangers?!

My life here at Belle Hills Farm is over. My world here has ended. Maybe I will have a life with a new mistress. But then my mind gently says to me, *Take heart, you are not alone in this. You will be with your momma and poppa.* The three of us will have to make our way together on the Overland Trail to a new world. We do not know what awaits us there. But somehow, this thought of the three of us, together, makes me somewhat calm.

CHAPTER THREE

Leaving Home

March 3, 1849, to April 2, 1849
Belle Hills Farm to St. Louis

March is usually a stormy month, but this day as we set our departure, it is calm and beautiful. The winds blow warm and softly around us. It makes me feel great sadness for the loss of my home and all I have ever known. Mistress says she will not accompany us to Charles Town. Instead, later today she will take the planned journey farther south to Richmond, Virginia, to bring Edward and Paul home. But Poppa says she will probably travel tomorrow as a journey such as that should begin in the earliest part of the day.

The morning of our departure, we arise so early, I scarce feel as if I have slept. Poppa's pallet has not been touched. I wonder if he stayed to the barn with the horses, or if he slept at all. I do not attend to Mistress. She does not call for me. I stay to the kitchen with Momma and Selby. Tawny and Sarah are in the kitchen with us preparing for the morning meal. They will take over our chores, though Mistress will have to do her own reading now. She has given Momma permission to take whatever cooking supplies, pots, and pans we might use on the journey. Though Poppa says when we arrive in Missouri, Mister Jason will be able to purchase proper cooking utensils suited for the trail.

Momma and I are packing crates when Mistress

enters the kitchen area. She greets us with only a nod as she inspects the simmering pots at the hearth and the morning bread cooling on the rack. She has a bundle wrapped in paper tucked under her arm. "This is ready-made fabric, for you to stitch sunbonnets for walking the trail," she says, handing it to Momma. Mistress surprises me with her remarks.

"You may be able to keep up your reading, Clementine. Maybe things are so wild and untamed on this road, no one will mind that you read or are able to write. Or maybe you will forget how to read? Do you have your little book?"

"Yes . . . No, mam . . . Yes," I say, nodding and sniffling back tears. "I will not forget." I do not know any other way or how to answer her or what to say to her. Her voice is sharp. Her words are crisp.

"You see to it that she reads, Adelaide." Momma nods. Mistress squeezes my shoulders and the top parts of both my arms. "You are strong, Clementine. You will need your strength for this journey."

She pauses. "Or should I call you Hope? You will need all that you have now and much more for what is in front of you. I will hold up my hope for all of you and your safe return."

Return? I think. The word rambles around in my head. I do not know what to do with the thoughts it brings to mind.

Then she turns to Momma.

"See to it that *he* eats—that *he* is well fed. You know how much he enjoys your cooking. You will need your strength too, Adelaide. Do you have your supplies of medicine herbs for sickness?"

"Yes, mam." Momma smiles and points to the crate where she keeps sacks and jars of dusty herbs, powders, brown leaves, tree bark, dried roots, and mixtures.

"Fare thee well, then," she says, tipping her head. Then she turns to Selby. "We do not have to set a formal breakfast table today. My appetite has not stirred. I think I will spend most of the day in my room until I travel to visit my sister later this afternoon if I do go this day. The weather is suited for travel today. It may not be tomorrow. With Jason gone, the house will be very empty now."

Then Poppa and Joseph come into the kitchen. They greet Mistress as is proper.

"Good morning, Mistress Barnett. We'll be traveling today."

"Yes," she replies. "I see it is perfect weather for that."

"I've come to start loading the wagon." He nods in her direction.

"Addy," he says to Momma. "What crates do you have ready to load? Joseph will take us to Charles Town."

Momma points out which ones to take.

"Just remember, Ezekiel," Mistress begins. "You remember what Mister Howard, Jason's father, would expect of you. It is up to you to keep him safe."

"Yes, mam. We will do what we can."

"Fare thee well, then." And she leaves the kitchen as quickly as she came in.

Later, everyone gathers on the porch and in the farmyard. Mister Uncle and Mistress appear on the portico as well. She calls to Mister Jason.

Mister Jason is dressed in a uniform. As a member of the company, he is to wear a short frock coat, single-breasted with gilded eagle buttons, and pantaloons of the same color, but there is a black stripe on the outer edge of both pant legs. The initials VCMC are on the front of his jacket. Because Poppa serves Mister Jason, he will wear only the short frock coat.

"My son, come near to me," Mistress calls again. She is holding another parcel in her hand. "You look very fine—so handsome. Your father would be proud to look upon you." She sniffles. "Here is a hymn book and your father's Bible. He would want you to have it. I want you to have it too. Read it every day. If you get too tired, have Hope read to you."

"Yes, Mother," he says moving into her arms in a warm embrace.

"I would rather give you a whole gold mine than have you leave me today."

"Mother, it is for the best," he says, and gives her a great and lasting hug. "I am only sorry that my dear brothers are far from home. But rest assured, Mother, I did tell them of my plans. I have their blessings as well. I will write to you as soon as I am able."

Then he turns stiffly to Mister Uncle.

"Good-bye, Uncle," he says extending his hand. "I offer my hand as a gesture of friendship and our family bond." With that, Jason turns away quickly.

With the wagon loaded, we set out for the train station at Harpers Ferry, Virginia. Momma and I packed enough food for the journey, but I am too tired to be hungry and yet I cannot settle myself down. I feel as though I am living in a dream of someone else's life that I am reading about in one of Mistress's books.

Poppa and Mister Jason sit in the driver's seat. Poppa drives the wagon. Momma, Joseph, and I sit inside the wagon with our luggage and supplies. Joseph will ride with us as far as Charles Town, Virginia. Then he will take the wagon back to Belle Hills Farm. I feel for my volume of poems in the pocket of my dress.

"Giddy-up," Poppa says, clicking his tongue to the horses. I turn to look back at Mistress probably for the last time and wave. She is not on the porch. Only

Mister Uncle and a few others remain there and in the yard. I do not feel compelled to wave to them. I clutch my little volume of poems.

I cannot say where my mind is. It seems not to be inside my body. It seems to be wandering somewhere above me with the clouds to places I never knew existed. We are on our way to Charles Town, Virginia. From Charles Town there is a special train that will take us to Harpers Ferry.

I believe I am already seeing the elephant. The locomotive train is a most powerful thing. Steel and iron have been molded and shaped to create a machine that moves across the road. It runs on steam. It is enormous. For all its power it is as loud—as loud as thunder rolls that shake the house and the very ground where it stands. It makes my heart beat fast just to be near to it.

But before we can board the locomotive train, Mister Jason and Poppa have to complete the last part of the process to join this company. They both have to sign the Memorandum of Agreement. Mister Walter, who is to serve as second-in-command, calls to the men to come near. Mister Cooper saves this most important part of the journey for this moment of embarkment.

"By now, you have pondered this journey and its

requirements. If you have any doubt in your minds," he tells the men gathered around him, "now is the moment to bow out. But if you place your signature or your mark here, there is no turning back, no matter how much disagreement you have about what decisions I make along this trail.

"No one is forcing you. With me, you travel of your own free will, and if you do so, there is no turning back from here. I will only let you out of the contract through grave sickness or death. Yours, not mine," he chuckles. Those words seem to relieve some of the building tension. And laughter rises around.

Then Mister Walter has each man on the trail line up single file for their turn to place their signature on the paper. Poppa has to do so too. Mister Jason demands this. Poppa stands right behind Mister Jason instead of having to go to the end of the line.

I never knew my life could be anything like this. I thought the excitement of the stories Mistress read to me, which filled me in an indescribable way, could only be found in books. But nothing can compare to taking the actual journey itself. I did not think my eyes and ears were enough to take in all I see and hear.

All around there is a crush of noise—a chorus of voices coming from such crowds of people, machines, animals—neighing horses, barking dogs. Suddenly a feeling of fear rushes over me. I am afraid I might be separated from Momma. I keep myself so close to her I make her misstep.

Joseph helps us put our baggage aboard the baggage car.

"You be careful with yourselves," he says. "We all at Belle Hills will keep a good thought out for you. Whether you return or not, be at peace with yourselves."

Hearing Joseph's calming words soothes me at the same time my thought of what is ahead races through my mind. And there is that word again—if we will *return*. It holds around me like a cloud—as big and heavy a weight as the steam train.

The train is so big, so powerful, and so loud. I wonder how anyone can keep their wits about them with all the noise and confusion around us. I never knew *anything* could be as big as it. And now I am to ride inside it. Poppa helps Momma and me get our crates settled in the baggage car. Then he leaves us to see to it that Mister Jason takes his seat before he rejoins us. We are not allowed to sit in the passenger car.

My heart races. The engine starts puffing up with steam quicker and quicker. I look around for Poppa.

A bell sounds again and again. *Clang, clang, clang.* The conductor calls, "All aboard. All aboard." *Where is Poppa? Where is Poppa?* I wonder. My throat feels as if it is closing up. The wheels begin turning, and Poppa appears jogging alongside the slow-moving train. Then he jumps in through the door of the train car to us. We all three sit huddled like that until the engine comes to its natural stop. All the while, I dare not speak. I do not know what to say or if I could be heard over the rattling thunder. I can only sit, holding Momma and Poppa close.

At Harpers Ferry the crowd is bigger. But where we stop everything is bigger and noisier. Almost as soon as we arrive, we board another train. This is the Baltimore and Ohio Railroad, Mister Walter tells us. It will take us up into the Allegheny Mountains of Maryland to the city of Cumberland, Maryland. Here we stop to stay and sleep overnight. The people of the company sleep in a hotel. Poppa, Momma, and I, like the other servants, find our sleeping quarters in a nearby barn. I am happy not to be moving.

The morning has us traveling again, this time by stagecoaches.

I count nine stagecoaches. Each has nine passengers packed tightly together. Our coach is somewhere at the front of the line. It is a lively ride down the mountain, but somehow I manage to fall asleep for the whole journey. By sundown we eventually reach a place called Brownsville on the Ohio River.

Momma says it was like I was a baby all over again. One by one the others arrive. Supper has been ordered and arranged for the company, including Momma, Poppa, and me. This is where I finally find a hearty appetite and am supposed to sleep. But I hardly sleep. Momma and I spend most of the night talking of all she witnessed during our trip over the mountains.

"We moved so fast. The countryside and this world are so beautiful. It is as if I never had eyes to see it this way before. It was as if the wind was pushing pictures of the world around for us to see," Momma says. Her voice sounds easy and bright. I think of Momma's words. As frightened as I am there is a growing peace inside me that is calm and full of myself, as I sit with Poppa and Momma.

The morning we land at Brownsville on the Ohio River I discover we are to travel not on land but on water—on a boat that is powered by steam! When we arrive, there is another great crush of even more people traveling and with them are all of their worldly possessions. They are waiting in a long line to board the steamboat the *White Cloud*. What a beautiful name for this boat. We are to take the *Robert Campbell*, another steamboat, which is standing and waiting for us to board. Already, the decks of both boats are filled with wagons, mules, oxen, mining equipment, and supplies in boxes and barrels. Despite all my fears, I am full of wonderment and awe. My mind moves so fast, trying to catch up to what surrounds me.

These boats are marvelous inventions, just like the locomotive. Amazing that they move on the same power of steam. To my eyes, the steamer resembles a house as huge as Belle Hills that sits upon the river. At one end there are many paddles that move, pushing it along the water. All are bound for St. Louis. We take passage on the *Robert Campbell* and run into another company on their way to California. There is a band of musicians on the boat. I enjoy the happy music. They play and sing the song "Oh! Susannah!" but they change the words:

"Oh! Susannah! Oh, don't you cry for me.
I'm bound for Cal-I forn-y
with my banjo on my knee."

I allow myself to feel some joy and relief. It does seem we have much to be happy about and a time to celebrate . . . if only for these moments. We all have arrived safely to this point and there is so much more up ahead.

"I do not know how this could be happening," I say to Momma. It is late morning, and we're preparing to eat the first meal of the day. "At once I am fearful only to be full of a feeling of excitement. Everything all around us is new. Everything around us is unexpected. Nothing can prepare us for what is up ahead." I do not know if she hears me. Momma's face seems calm and more at peace than I ever saw her before.

"I understand your meaning," Momma finally says. "As fearful as I am about this journey with both you and Poppa, I feel a hope I have never known before. Something new stirs inside of me.

"Yes, the travel is harder work than that inside Belle Hills. There are no walls around us here—only wide-open spaces. We are surrounded by strangers. All along our journey there has been talk and murmurs of sickness and disease. Cholera. And there are still dangers we cannot imagine. But it occurs to me that in some of all of this I can feel a newness I never had before. I will learn and discover new things. Your poppa feels the way I do."

I look at Momma. I have never heard her speak like this. But I feel this way as well.

"I thought Belle Hills was all of the world and the only world. We know what that world is like. Maybe the one where we are going is worse and worser along the way. Or maybe it is all the same for us. Maybe it is the same as this but for a while, we will breathe new air, Hope. Not Virginia air. Not Belle Hills air, but another kind of air—air of the wilderness . . . ," she says, pausing and speaking again.

"They tell me there are a lot of new kinds of people all along the way of where we are going. I feel happy to be seeing them."

Then a warm wind blows, swirling around us. I think maybe for now it is enough for Momma and me to just notice this new air.

"Smell this air. And keep your eyes open for new things to see. Mister Jason calls it seeing the elephant," Momma says, and she laughs a laugh I have never heard her laugh before. "Maybe for now that is how we have to view things until we know more and can see more of what is ahead. I feel strong, my daughter. We will look for the elephants along the way." She laughs again. "Look for the elephants," she murmurs to herself, laughing. "You stay strong in this with my hope, my daughter—of seeing all things new."

Huddled on the deck of the steamer, we watch the sights and sounds of this brand-new world coming and going around us.

"This is America too, my daughter. It is bigger and stranger than what we have known so far. Maybe somewhere in all of this bigness there can be a place for all of us. Look at these wide-open spaces. It fills up empty spaces inside the mind."

CHAPTER FOUR

Beginning the Trail to the New World

April 2, 1849, to May 11, 1849
The St. Louis Riverfront
St. Louis, Missouri

Finally, we arrive safely at St. Louis. St. Louis!

"I declare," Momma says. "I counted about four weeks of days since we left. It feels that I have lived a lifetime in that we have traveled. This is a whole other world than Belle Hills."

Momma is right. I feel as though I have lost all track of time. At home I knew by my chores, what to do each day—each second. Now it seems as though I am living in the wildest of dreams, where time cannot be measured in the same way.

This city looks very beautiful from the river. Up close it looks to be bursting at its seams. It is a mixture—a collection of things. It is a port, a modern city, and lastly, in ways, a very rough country. Momma and I stand on the deck of the *Robert Campbell* as it is coming into this waterfront town. As we pull into the harbor, one side of the riverbank is lined with countless steamboats. Each one is loaded with freight and passengers. The air is clogged with smoke from puffing steamboats. Cargo and supplies are piled up waiting to be loaded onto the boats. There is so much noise. Many frustrations arise, and swears. Mister Walter warns us there could be crooks and thieves among the crowd. It seems there is a contest between each steamer for space along the dock and who can make the greater racket.

Those boats that are docked are discharging the freight they carried and the passengers. Heavy footsteps thud down the gangplank and people in the excited mob have to yell even louder just to be heard.

There are men on horses, people on foot, men and women and children all packed from the water up to the street. Crowds of people are of every color from every different land. There are languages—sounds of words I have never heard spoken. There are thudding sounds of heavy flour barrels being rolled down the ramp, the whinnying noise of horses and braying sounds of donkeys and their hooves on the pavement. There is the rattling of wagons and the creaking sound of their wheels. The number of people has increased. Many merchants are here to sell their wares. Where could they all be coming from?

There are storehouses here to purchase supplies, but some of the merchants come to the street area to shout out their products. It is hard to listen to everything and make sense of all that goes on. I wonder if it is ever quiet here.

On placards and papers there are advertisements for supplies and so many things the emigrants who are bound for California and Oregon must have. For the California bound, every emigrant must have a special gold washer. Momma asks me to read what the placard papers say.

"'Certain kinds of flours are better than others for the trail. We have them all here. Don't miss your chance to buy.'" There is a picture of a sack of flour. Momma loses interest in the sign. We look across the river.

On the other side of the river three deer stand on a little hill, a mound of earth. Someone from the dock shoots at them, but they do not stir. The deer do not run. They slowly walk away.

"They call this Mound City," Mister Walter says, pointing to where we saw the deer.

"See those large hilly places above the Missouri River?" He points. Momma and I stare. They look like simple little hills. There are about eight or nine of them rounded at the top. Another is very large and flat topped.

"There, on the other side of the riverbank where we saw the deer, are the mounds or hills of earth where the Osage people have their homes and lives.

"They are a peaceful people," Mister Walter says. "They are skilled hunters, farming people, and warriors if they need to be." The Osage people stand quiet and still, collected there along dotted bluffs, watching the movement and hearing commotion taking place.

"Those mounds were built from the earth long

before the European people came here. Long ago this was home to many—different tribes made up of the first people who lived here. Once they were one people—there were Omahas, Ponkas, Osage, and Kansas...."

Mister Walter stops suddenly. I think he wants to tell us more. I want him to, but Mister Cooper calls out for assistance. Mister Walter is needed to help with the cargo. This side of the river, across from the early mounds, has mounds too. But these are giant heaps and piles and stacks of people and things growing larger and larger—some unimaginable.

The eye cannot take in all that it needs to see fast enough for the mind to understand. Both sides of the river are peppered with white tents and wagons of emigrants. Already this port city is highly populated. There is much industry. And yet, I think of Mister Uncle's cousin, who must live right near this very place where we stand. With thoughts of this cousin, I wonder about returning before we even start. I wonder if this place will be our new home. But those thoughts will have to wait. There is much to do.

"Look around and see what's here. St. Louis is the best place to get our provisions and supplies," Mister Cooper tells us. "The farther away from civilization we go, the higher the cost of things we will need for the journey."

"Maybe the paper about the flour was right after all," Momma whispers to me. When we see Mister Jason again, Momma asks him to pay special attention to this. We need good flour.

The supplies and provisions purchased here will be ferried separately on to Independence, just up the river. It is difficult enough. Mister Jason and Poppa go to search for places to buy the things we will need. Momma and I are instructed to wait where we are until they return. I do not mind this as there is much I want to see. Everything startles the imagination.

Much farther down the river are two scows, or flatboats. They ferry the emigrants, their supplies, and possessions across the river. We hear people passing by us say that these boats are used from early in the morning until past midnight each day. There is much to do before we are ready to cross. We must outfit our wagon with supplies. Mister Walter warned us before reaching our jumping-off point there will be much waiting around. Everything moves by inches.

Momma and I sit with our luggage and crates. We cannot help to hear something happening at the courthouse several streets into the city. There, we are told, a large crowd is gathering. Already, Momma and I have made up our minds about this city. We will be happy to move on. As we settle ourselves, we hear the sounds of moans, screams, yells, and cries. I suddenly feel sick—a growing terror rises inside me.

Later we hear that an auction is going on at the Old Courthouse. My fear does not subside. I know they are selling people, too.

A sign is posted on the side of a building. It is a list of requirements for Negroes:

**RULES FOR NEGROES BY ORDER
OF THE CITY OF ST. LOUIS**

**THERE IS A CURFEW. OFF THE STREET BY 8:00 P.M.
MONDAY THROUGH FRIDAY
AND 11:00 P.M. SATURDAY AND SUNDAY.**

**IF CURFEW IS VIOLATED, THIRTY-NINE LASHES WILL
BE ADMINISTERED TO THE PERSON CHARGED AND AN
ADDITIONAL MONETARY CHARGE OF $1.00
FOR ROOM AND BOARD IN THE LYNCH SLAVE
PEN FOR THE NIGHT.**

ALL SLAVES MUST NOT—

READ OR WRITE

SMOKE IN PUBLIC

WALK WITH A CANE

RIDE IN A CARRIAGE (WITHOUT PERMISSION)

**ALL SLAVES AND FREE BLACKS MUST POSSESS A
PASS AT ALL TIMES. THOSE WITHOUT A PASS WILL BE
ARRESTED BY THE CITY POLICE. FOR THOSE FREE
BLACKS MOVING INTO MISSOURI AFTER 1847, YOU WILL
BE "REDUCED TO SLAVERY" IF YOU DO NOT LEAVE.**

When I read that the city of St. Louis punishes people like me who have my ability, my mind becomes a swirl of worry. Momma knows my uneasiness. She takes my hand and whispers to me, "Tell your mind, do not think so many thoughts." Then she hands me a bundle of cloth. "This is a good time now to stitch our head coverings." Momma smiles. I reach for the cloth, happy for this chore to steady me.

While I stitch, a thought comes to mind: how curious it is that if it is unlawful for the likes of me and my kind to read, how are those poor souls supposed to know these things?

A man approaches us. I am afraid but I do not feel it wise to show my fear. I must not. I take Momma's hand in order to speak to him. I do remember that I saw him when he came into our group in Brownsville. I saw him talking to Mister Cooper. I saw him signing his Memorandum of Agreement. He is one of the passengers from our company. I remember he had a terrible time of stomach sickness for most of the river journey. He smiles as he comes up to Momma and me to introduce himself.

"I am Jonathan Lincoln George. I see we are in the same group." He is friendly enough and we share our names.

"She is Adelaide." I point to Momma. "And I am Hope."

"I saw you on the steamer."

"Yes," I say. "And we saw you as well. Momma says . . . you should chew on peppermint leaves if you are prone to stomach upset." Then she reaches into her parcel. Mister George smiles.

"Keep these in your pocket, in case you have a need," Momma says, handing the leaves to him.

"Thank you." He chuckles, tucking them into his vest. "I am much obliged to you both. Where are you headed? Oregon? California?" he asks.

"We are headed to California with Mister Jason Barnett. Momma will cook for our wagon. I am to help with the cooking chores and launder our linens. My poppa is the one who tends the wagons and horses."

"So very nice to meet you both. I suppose it is good to be traveling with loved ones. I am traveling alone. I am a schoolteacher. I have been teaching in the South. And now I find myself in need of my own learning—something new for myself—an adventure! I plan to visit California, Texas, the New Mexico Territory, and perhaps even South America! I am studying law while I continue teaching. Eventually, I plan to settle in the west. And you? What are your plans?"

"I declare, Mister Jonathan Lincoln George, we cannot say. But we will travel with Mister Jason and help him to reach the gold mine diggings in California. That is our requirement," I say.

"What is occurring down the street is horrible," Mister George says, looking at Momma and me and pointing to where the noise is coming from. We only look away.

". . . but did you also know that within the walls of that very courthouse is where a landmark lawful decision is about to take place?"

"A lawful decision?" I ask.

"A man by the name of Dred Scott and his wife, Harriet Scott, took their futures into their own hands. I came to know of this event from reading the newspaper. Three years ago, in 1846, Scott and his wife came to this very place to make their plea to seek their freedom from enslavement. Dred Scott was born into enslavement in Virginia."

"Virginia?" I interrupt, putting my hand over my mouth.

"We are from that place as well," Momma adds.

"Well, this fifty-year-old man, upon having been brought here from Virginia with one family as servants, was to be sold to another family here in St. Louis."

When I hear these words, it brings to mind Mister Uncle's cousin. This time, I cannot keep the fear from rising.

"Mister Scott decided for himself to end this life of servitude. He filed suit against the family for his freedom, and it seems he may just win this case. The court has not made its decision as yet. It probably won't be settled for a while, but my hunch is he will win! At least, I hope so."

"You think he can *win* the case?" Momma asks.

"Yes, I believe he and his wife could be free," he says.

"So . . . it . . . could be possible that an enslaved person can manifest their destiny by gaining their freedom?" I ask.

Mister George looks at me and chuckles again.

"Yes, my dear Hope. It appears in the context of everything we are living in this hard and cruel world, there can come moments when someone is able to slip through the cracks and live the life they choose. That is why I am on this journey. This is what I plan to do—manifest *my* destiny to become a lawyer!" He chuckles again and waves as he goes on his way.

"I will see you again on our journey."

"I hope we will see Mister George again," I say to Momma.

I watch with wonder the sight of the hurrying crowd of emigrants all with one desire—to cross the river.

Now there is but one scow. I hope when it is our turn to cross, there will be space for us. The crowd continues to grow. Mister Cooper has been told it has been so for weeks. Many thousands are embarking on a journey west, And from the numbers of people here, this will continue for several weeks more.

Everything is in large numbers: mules, wagons, oxen, horses, cargo, boxes, barrels, and people all waiting. Nothing is still. Everything is growing and moving all the time. The animals have been placed in a corral nearby as everyone waits their turn. As soon as one group boards the boat, the next group must move down to the water's edge in place to wait their turn. For all the stirring chaos, life here is like a giant machine with many turning parts. The ferry continues just as the river flows.

Yet, for some, this waiting around causes great strain and tension. Someone shoots their firearm.

The next day, there is still only one ferry with hundreds of wagons waiting to cross. It takes time and patience to load the animals and equipment onto the boats. The waiting wagons in the long line stretch up into the heart of the town. Each holds their place, day and night. There is yelling and fights. Word came that someone was fatally shot.

The crowd is thick and the need to cross continues

to grow. As soon as a wagon enters the boat, another closes in down to the edge of the bank, and the long line of wagons slowly moves forward. All the waiting around causes frayed nerves and short tempers. This will go on from dawn to midnight, day after day, until sooner or later, our turn to board will come. For now, we must only be concerned with getting our outfitting supplies for the way west.

It is hard to keep track of the hours and days. Somehow, this is no concern. For now, the only concern is patience and to get across the river.

Today it is very, very hot. Mister Cooper says cholera is bad along the river. Late in the afternoon, we discover that Mister Jason has taken ill with the dreaded disease. Mister Jason has been taking his meals and sleeping at a boardinghouse since we arrived here in St. Louis.

"Momma said he should not have stepped one foot into that place at all," I whisper to Poppa.

Mister Jason returns to us with complaints of pressure over his stomach. He retches and heaves but can bring nothing up. He says he is burning up with fever. He aches in his head, but his bowels are not affected. Momma lays him down and puts hot stones wrapped in cloth on the soles of his feet and on parts of his body so he can sweat. Some other people in our company have come down with it. The doctor has gone on up the river to camp. Poppa goes to fetch him, but returns shortly to say the doctor cannot get back until the morning.

Momma refuses to allow Mister Jason to return to the boarding house tonight. Those from our company also complain about being "eaten up with bedbugs."

"I have the bites to prove it," one man says.

Poppa pitches Mister Jason's tent.

"Bring my remedy box," Momma tells me. She stays awake to nurse Mister Jason as it is no different from when he was a young one at Belle Hills. She will stay with him until the doctor can see to him. Mister Jason is resting sleepily.

"I wonder if we should worry," I whisper to Momma. They are saying some people do not survive cholera.

"Do not worry, daughter. My remedies are good for this, too," she says, smiling. Mister Jason is sleeping. As I start to leave the tent, Momma touches my arm. "Stay," she says, handing me a piece of paper. "Mister Jason gave this to me. It is a paper about the flour. What does it say?"

"It says," I begin, "'Flour Especially for the California and Oregon Emigrants.'"

I feel safe inside the tent with Momma and Mister Jason. The light is not very good, but I am able to read the paper. No one in St. Louis can see me using my gift as I read these things to her.

The next morning when the doctor finally arrives, Mister Jason appears to be resting easily. Doctor Tillman examines Mister Jason.

"This man is on the mend. My help is not needed here. He will recover." He looks at Momma, who is sitting at Mister Jason's bedside.

"I thought they said this man was sick with cholera. Did you do this?" he asks with a friendly smile, looking directly at Momma.

"Yes," she whispers.

"Well, he owes you a debt." A look comes over Momma's face I have never seen before. It is a look I will never forget. "We lost three men last night," the doctor says. "Because of you, we did not lose a fourth one."

Mister Cooper has placed several men as guards for the Virginia California Mining Company encampment. There is a sprawl of tents and wagons and much to do. There is no need to rush now. We are waiting for the prairie trails to dry out from the spring rains. The company is using this time to make purchases for the trip ahead.

It is agreed to buy as much of what we need here in St. Louis rather than Independence. There are stories told of troubles at the next point of our journey. Mister Cooper has sent men ahead as scouts to determine the truth of these tales.

Mister Cooper and Mister Walter know the country very well. They know many of these traders and merchants who outfit the wagon trains. Our guides remind us of which of the sellers are trustworthy and of the best places to buy.

Now that Mister Jason is feeling better, he and Poppa will go looking to buy what we need. Here, there are dozens of blacksmiths, wheelwrights, wagonmakers, and outfitting shops.

Last night at supper Mister Jason and Poppa talked about what to look for in the wagon. Poppa said the wagon should be the simplest possible construction—strong, lightweight, and made of well-seasoned timber—especially the wheels. Poppa said the wheelwright merchant talked about how the air temperature will change and dry out worse than in Virginia. The wheels will need constant repairs to prevent them from falling to pieces. Poppa is looking to buy wheels made from Osage wood. Momma and I were busy organizing what supplies we already have, but my mind did not stay on those chores. I so want to see the draft animals we will purchase.

I looked to Momma and then to Poppa. "May I come along?"

But Mister Jason answered first. "If only your Mistress could see that you are turning from a lady's maid to an adventurer . . . an argonaut!" He laughed.

The wagon is only for carrying the things we need to survive in the wilderness. It holds our bedding, food provisions, utensils for cooking, and tools for repairs. Even so, it will not be big enough to carry everything for the whole trip. We must carry water. There are stopping points—military forts—along the way to resupply what we need. No one will ride on the wagon unless there is sickness. We are to walk the whole way alongside it to lead the draft animals. After Mister Jason and Poppa are satisfied with the kind of wagon and order it, we must find the animals.

Mister Jason is kind to remember how his father, Mister Clinton Barnett, depended on Poppa regarding the horses and the wagons. Mister Uncle saw his worth too.

One of the company, Charles Ferbridge, chastises Mister Jason for relying on Poppa. "You will allow him to make such a decision?"

"I can do no other thing," Mister Jason says, standing up straight and stiffening his back. "Ezekiel is a loyal and devoted servant in my family. My dearly departed father trusted him with our horses and wagons. I have no reason not to now."

The man says no more.

The decision on which kind of draft animal to use to pull the wagon is a most important one. Poppa is thinking on the prospect of using oxen. He says they are steady and strong animals and that he likes their calm and gentle disposition. And they can be used for food if need be. Mules will be used for pack animals.

Outside of the mercantile supply store is where the draft animals are purchased. Mister Cooper introduces the trader to Mister Jason and Poppa. He has brought the animals up from Mexico along the Santa Fe Trail. Mister Cooper is confident in the man who sells the oxen. He says buying from him, we will get a good, healthy team. He is Mister Fernando Becerra. He will only sell oxen and mules. He says horses are not suited for *el camino*, such a journey. The animals he sells are already broken in on prairie grasses and accustomed to being yoked. They arrived here weeks ago and are rested for this long walk ahead of us.

Poppa is happy when he looks over the animals. He sees they are well cared for. He tells Mister Jason we should purchase twelve oxen. The price is set at thirteen dollars each. Mister Walter says this is a fair price. They will be paired and yoked when pulling the wagon. Oxen must wear shoes to protect their hooves. Mister Becerra says they should have new shoes for the new journey. Poppa wants to help with the shoeing. First, he watches Mister Becerra and how he talks kindly to each animal as he lifts its foot. He speaks in English as he tells it what he is doing. And he sings while he works.

"They like your singing," Poppa says to Mister Becerra.

"Si," he says. "I always speak and sing to them in your language so they will understand what you say. Singing and talking sweetly around them calms them. Take care of these beasts. They will be great friends to you along the trail."

Then Poppa tries singing the song. "Mary had a little lamb ...," he begins. His voice is deep. The oxen bellow softly. Poppa laughs his hearty laugh.

Next, Poppa looks over the mules. He talks with Mister Becerra and Mister Jason. Poppa says he thinks six will be enough. He tells Mister Jason we should practice with the animals hitched up to the wagon so that they will be used to the work on the trail. Mister Jason never had to worry about these things while we lived at Belle Hills. He decides to help Poppa with the training.

While we are here in St. Louis, we must also buy the tools we need to make repairs on the wagon, cooking utensils, and provisions we will eat—sugar, salt, pepper, bacon, butter, lard, tea, coffee, flour, vinegar, dried beans, rice, dried fruit, potatoes, turnips, a whole keg of pickles, saleratus, molasses—so many things to stock our pantry. Momma asks Mister Jason to make sure to get a nice-sized bucket for the leftover grease, a water bucket, a water barrel, a coffee pot, a Dutch oven—a big pot with a lid to use for making stews or baking bread—other cooking utensils, knives, forks, spoons, and plates that are made of tin.

We are told later that perhaps next week, while we wait for the ground to dry from the spring rains, the company will be able to ferry our wagons, supplies, and animals up the river to our jumping-off point.

Mister Jason and Poppa are pleased with the choice of wagon, called a prairie schooner. Because the wagon has a wide bed, or bottom, it has a shape much like a boat. We can fit many provisions here. This wagon is made this way for moving across rivers when needed. The canvas cover is called a bonnet and is very much like the head covering we women have to wear to protect us from the hot sun. The open end of these covers can be closed and tied up tight to keep out the dust from the road.

Some who plan to live in California have brought all of their worldly and household possessions—clothing, china, furniture—things that are very beautiful and too delicate or heavy for this rough road.

"Too many things," Mister Cooper says. "The path to California is strewn with an abundance of those things. Once we get moving on the trail, people will see they can only afford to bring those things that are necessities. Many of their belongings will be abandoned and left along the way." In all, this train has sixteen wagons—we will only use one wagon.

There is a corral where the horses and mules are kept. Oxen are put in a pen to themselves. For the time we are in St. Louis, nearly every day some team runs off and causes an upset. Some of the mules are wild and have to learn to be tame to travel well.

The next task for Poppa and Mister Jason, while we wait our turn to leave for the jumping-off point, is to get the mules ready. First, Poppa puts them to our wagon to break them. Then he ties the animal's halter to the back wheel for some time to get them to be gentle enough to wear the harness. I understand now what Mister Clinton thought of my poppa and his knowledge of the animals that pull our wagons.

"When it comes to the care and feeding of horses and wagons, Ezekiel has more than horse sense." He would laugh the many times he told Mistress this fact. Mister Jason remembers to Momma and me how Poppa was depended on in these matters. Mister Jason is pleased with the decisions Poppa has made. I only wish Mistress and Mister Howard could see their son and how well he is suited for this adventure.

The morning temperatures are usually cool, but it grows to boiling quickly by the middle of the day.

The hot days add to the unrest and irritability of the people in our company.

The strain and fears of the trip set in long ago. Already, before we embark on the wilderness trail, two members of the company talk of going no farther. They argue that they will not take one step more.

"Let us stop right here. Start a colony. And settle here in this very place—in this beautiful country." But that suggestion is wildly and noisily opposed by the majority of the group. And to ease the pressure, someone in the wagon train breaks out in song and dance. Then, everyone starts singing,

"California, that's the land for me.
I'm bound for California with a washbowl on my knee!"

My mind wanders, thinking on these things. It is no doubt beautiful country, but all I can think of is Mister Uncle's cousin who lives nearby. I too am fearful, but I am most eager to leave this place and start the trail.

Our captain will not hear of their idea to stay put. He calls all the men together. The women and children come too, though we stay toward the back of the company.

"You signed on to this journey. I have your signatures and your promise. Remember that. I will need every able-bodied one of you here to make this journey forward. The matter is settled. We move onward to California."

Then he has the wagons numbered. We are wagon number nine. Mister Cooper further gives orders that each one is to fall in line by number. We drive with what they called check lines—straps of leather that attach to the wagon in front of you to keep space between the animals so the poor beasts do not breathe in so much of the trail dust.

Mister Cooper tells the men, "Yes. This is a long journey. And it is a hard one." He looks around at the people in his company. He looks them in their eyes.

"Many of you may not make it. But the chances of you making it to this new and promised land are very good. Just keep your wits about you. As we wait our turn on the ferry, consider this: Let us go forth, together, with one accord."

All night a boat is grounded on land bars and running afoul of snags.

Finally, Poppa thinks there is hope. It is only seven or eight hours more before we board the ferry. Still, it is a long time to wait. There is much excitement and anticipation floating in the air around us.

At last, it is our turn to board the steamer. Mister Cooper tells us has he sent several men ahead of our main group to make a camp for our arrival in Independence.

When I hear these words, my heart is glad.

At 8:00 in the morning, our company and supplies are loaded onto the steamer the *Anna Mae* to ferry up the Missouri River. There is much noise and activity to load our cargo. Finally, we are crowded and aboard the steamer. Every space above and below deck are filled. Mister Walter says we are lucky. Most of the passengers are from our group, the VCMC. It takes five to six days to reach our destination.

CHAPTER FIVE

Traveling with Wagons, Mules, Oxen, Dogs, and Men

May 12, 1849, to June 10, 1849
Independence, Missouri, to Fort Kearny

The Missouri is much like the roads back home. It is a river highway. All day and night, up and down the river, boats come and go to load and unload passengers, animals, and cargo. Independence is where the three roads west come together—the Oregon, California, and Santa Fe Trails. At first, the sight of it is very different from St. Louis. There is no port or dock here. No streets or buildings. There is just a stretch of land. This is what they call the Lower Landing. But the piles of cargo and barrels are the same. They sit at the shoreline, waiting to be loaded onto the steamer. Encampments of emigrants and wagon companies are spread out far and wide. People sit surrounding their campfires.

Above and to the left of the Lower Landing is a pathway up a steep hill. The path is lined with trees and bushes on both sides. As we come closer to the shore, three wagons climb the hill to the Upper Landing. The hilly area of the Upper Landing looks like a wilderness.

In the early morning hours of the fifth day, our boat slows and comes to a stop. Everyone on board the steamer cheers. I am happy to get away from the tight, crowded spaces of the boat. The ground is sandy and damp. It is the Lower Landing. The city of Independence resides on the Upper Landing, six miles or so away. I am glad to hear it is a modern, busy town, full of industry, like St. Louis.

We unload from the ferry, and our company quickly prepares for the move to the Upper Landing. When we get to our encampment, we are glad to see John Hutchinson and Thomas Bailey, men who were sent ahead to mark off a camping area for our company.

There is much work ahead of us before we can rest. We move the animals into large pens and feed and water them. We stack our cargo and equipment. We work as quickly as we can. Everyone is weary. Momma starts our cooking fire, and Poppa and Mister Jason raise our tents. Our guides tell us we will camp here for some days to make sure the animals are travel-ready and to wait for the new prairie grasses to grow while the ground dries up from the heavy spring rains.

There is a report that someone in our camp has died. It is sad news to hear it is a grandfather. But we are relieved it is a natural death and not from cholera. We cannot move on until he has been laid to rest. The men must dig the grave and make the hole very deep. Heavy rocks are found to place on the burial spot so wild animals will not find it.

We hear more news of cholera from Thomas Bailey. It is bad all along the river. At this meal, Momma feeds us extra pickles and adds cayenne pepper to the food. The taste takes some getting used to, but she says it may help to keep us in good health. I only am glad this day has come to an end.

I awake to the sound of birds and the smell of bacon. Some of the men have gone into Independence to see what else they may buy. I declare I like the sound of the word. I am glad to hear it is an outfitting town too. We will remain here for a while until Mister Cooper thinks the time is right to start the trail. In the meantime, we rest and prepare.

After breakfast Poppa and Mister Jason go into the city of Independence to look around. Mister Jason is being especially nice to Momma. He asks her if she would like some special thing from town. Momma giggles at the thought. Poppa tells me Mister Jason is feeling good and thankful to Momma. He is grateful to be well and alive.

Momma and I use this time for washing clothes. It is a hard job leaning over the river. The water is very cold. It freezes the hands to stiffness. We pass the one bar of lye soap back and forth over each garment and scrub by rubbing the two sides of the garment together with our hands. I think of how particular

Mistress was in her clothing and appearance. I think of how I am supposed to dress at Belle Hills. I wonder if she would think of all my training as a lady's maid was being wasted. And I am grateful Mistress is not here to see how clothes do not come as clean as when we were home.

For each garment, Momma takes one end, I take another, and we twist hard, going in opposite directions. This way we get as much of the water out as we can. Poppa has placed sticks in the ground close to the fire. We hope the clothes will be dry before too long. Momma gives me bacon grease to smear on my cold and sore hands, but it does not help much.

Mister Jason and Poppa return from town late in the day around suppertime. They are full of stories.

"The prices are not much higher." Mister Jason talks excitedly. "But that animal trader asks twice the price we paid Mister Becerra for oxen," he tells us.

Poppa agrees.

Mister Jason tells us he is happy we did not wait to buy our supplies and goods here. He hands Momma a little tin. "This is for you, Adelaide."

"Sardines?!" Momma smiles.

"I know you prefer oysters, but so far from our beloved Chesapeake, they are hard to come by here."

"This is plenty good enough," Momma says. "I am much obliged to you."

"They tell us the inhabitants of Independence do not do well," Mister Jason says. "Cholera rages.

"There are many emigrants here," Mister Jason starts again. "Emigrants of every type fill the street. We met several French men, mountain men. They are hunters and trappers. They keep their hair long and wear buckskin clothes. I may like to have a suit of clothing such as that." He laughs.

"Here, just as in St. Louis, everyone is in a hurry. Tensions and nerves are just as high. When tempers flare into fights, there is what is called frontier justice.

"If someone breaks the law, they are to pay a fine and spend the night in jail, which is a small log cabin with only a door and a window. This allows the fellow to cool off and stay out of trouble."

There are some men who still are not attached to a wagon company. They seem most miserable. Our captains are leery of these people and feel they cannot be trusted. We are told to steer clear of them. The time for signing on was weeks ago. I am glad we already are attached to Mister Cooper's group, the VCMC.

Here in our company are squabbles, harsh words, and threats. Now there is an argument and disagreement on the subject of dogs. Two families want a meeting about this.

Some families brought their beloved pets. Then there are those that feel these animals will be more than a nuisance. I am too tired to listen and attend to all the reasons. I fall asleep. By morning, I awake to a strangeness around me. For our company everyone is quiet. It was decided that dogs would not be allowed to travel with us. I do not know what happened to the dogs, but no sound of barking can be heard.

After a breakfast of bacon, bread, and hot coffee with extra sugar, Momma whispers to me and motions for me to follow her. We walk beyond the trees to a clearing.

"Daughter, look around you," she says softly, taking in deep breaths of air. "Spring is here in this land. These flowers are so beautiful. And I see some plantings as the ones that grow at Belle Hills. Help me with my gathering." Momma and I walk along over the fields. We do not stray too far from camp. Out in the open prairie, there are many different types of grasses and flowers growing.

"I want to gather some of the plants," she says. "The ones I know. This is purple clover. This is good for almost anything—any ailment." In another part of the field, she finds another plant for picking.

This night there is a wild storm. Rain with thunder and lightning. The sound is deafening. I am at once frightened by it but also full of wonder and surprise at everything in this new world. Mister Jason and Poppa are tending the animals. They will remain with them so they are not frightened by the storm. Momma and I are not able to sleep under a tent very well. It is a hard soaking rain. We constructed a make-shift tent from the extra oilcloth we bought in St. Louis to put over the wagon to help keep it dry. We climb inside the wagon. It is crowded with all of our supplies. Somehow, we manage to sleep.

What I am left with in my thoughts is the scent of the rainstorm coming. All at once the smell of dry dirt fills my nose as when Joseph turns the soil in the field. But something else in the air is so heavy and full, it spills over upon me, telling me this place is nothing like home at Belle Hills. And for the first time in such a long forever while, I think of my little book. I do not bring it out of its dry protected place into this pouring rain. But when I close my eyes, listening to the sound of water falling, I imagine I am seeing the words on the page. It is a comfort.

Today and well into the next day, Mister Cooper talks about what to expect our life on the prairie will be after leaving the Missouri River. The men take turns to stand guard every night we camp. Each will pair with another to watch over the livestock.

There have been stories of horses and mules being stolen. Poppa laughs because the thieves do not care for the oxen.

There continues to be so much confusion and so much for my eyes to view I can scarcely keep my wits about me. There is the sound of gunshot from somewhere behind us from another wagon company. We are told there was an injury. Later, before we sleep this night, Mister Cooper calls his company together in a voice different than he has used before.

"This journey will change you. Whoever you are and whatever you started out to be at the beginning of this journey, these plains we are about to cross will change you. And that is good. You will come out of this more than who you know yourself to be if you allow it. The road up ahead will require that and more of you.

"Watch your tempers," he speaks almost in a yell. "I say this again! Watch. *Your. Own.* Tempers. Nobody else's! This is a hard journey. You are apt to become more irritable and ill-natured with each passing day. Watch your tempers.

"That man who exercises the greatest forbearance under such circumstances, who remains cheerful, slow to take up quarrels, and endeavors to reconcile difficulties among his companions, is deserving of all praise and goodwill, without doubt, for he will contribute greatly to the success and comfort of this expedition.

"This is all I will speak of these things. I am telling you this now so that you will know for the times up ahead."

All I can do is take these words in. Somehow I feel they make me grow larger inside myself. This life I am in now—it is nothing like the life I lived with Mistress at Belle Hills Farm. I feel I am in charge of me, of my own dear self.

At Belle Hills Momma hardly spoke. Here on the trail as tired as she is, she seems revived and is showing a side of herself I never knew was there. Mister Cooper is right. This road to California changes you.

Mister Cooper tells us there are over two thousand miles of wilderness, prairie, desert, and mountains that lie before us between the state of Missouri where we stand and the Pacific Ocean. We will travel more than three hundred miles to reach Fort Kearny. Our provisions must last until then. He tells us what the daily schedule will be.

Each day will begin as early as 4:00 a.m. At the sound of a bugle call we awake. Quickly we have breakfast, break camp, and we are to be on the road by 5:00 or 6:00 a.m. We walk until nooning time, when we stop to eat. Then we are on the road again until about 5:00 or 6:00 p.m. With this schedule he hopes we can travel fifteen to twenty miles per day.

"It is good we are on the road at the time in the year when daylight grows, and nighttime shortens," Momma says.

This morning, Mister Cooper starts the trail. The bugle begins our day. We must be fed, packed, and ready when we get the call to move. We do not want to be left behind. This road to California is very busy. There are many other companies traveling along this way for the same destination. All wagons have their place. Each group stands at the ready for the call to head out. Mister Jason moves around our wagon with Poppa to give things one last check. Momma and I stand with the wagon. Mister Cooper yells.

"Move out!" He rides his horse up and down the wagon train. "Let's get going!"

And now, the march begins.

"Good-bye, civilization!" someone utters aloud. "Hello, wilderness!" And then there is laughter.

Slowly the oxen teams begin their march. The wheels of the prairie schooner turn. The wooden wagons rattle and creak and squeak while their bonnets sway from side to side. Yes, our adventure journey has begun.

"Most of this land was where the Chickasaw,

Delaware, Otoe, Osage, Quapaw, Fox, and Shawnee lived—I don't know all their names," Mister Walter says as he stretches out his hand over the land to point. "Back in 1830 the government made a law that removed those tribes. They can't feel too good about that. But most are friendly."

Voices of gossip and worry rise up like the thick dust from the path. First, there are questions of safety. Daily there are frightening stories and questions about how we can survive. Can we be protected in this wilderness? Then comes worry over whether our captain will lead us off course. I try to close my ears to keep from hearing the awful complaints. Already there is enough for a mind to think about; just putting one foot in front of the other is quite difficult. The ground is uneven. In some places it is still soft and wet from the rains. In other spots it is dry. You must be careful where you step. Stumbling happens easily.

We push out into the open country beyond, our long line of "prairie schooners" crossing this well-traveled unsteady road. So many others who have gone here before us have left the road broken and rough, marked by juts and bumps and grooves from their wagon wheels, feet, and animal hooves.

A large bird flies overhead. Its shadow moves across the ground. For a moment, I wonder what it all looks like from high up above our heads as we move onto the green and billowy landscape. I turn to look back from where we had come—but only see the other end of the wagon train.

Again, I remember my mistress. I remember that day so long ago when I turned hoping to look on her and see her one last time. But she was not standing on the porch. It makes my mind wonder if I should remember that. Do not look back over where I had come hoping for what I think would be there. "Only forward," I mumble to myself. "Let this road change you."

All along this way I try to be as small and unnoticed as can be. I complete my clothes-washing chores, my cooking chores with Momma, and do my best to keep my mind still.

"There is much dullness in these miles up ahead," Mister Walter announces. This causes my mind to wander, remembering the frightful stories of St. Louis, and I am glad to be moving on.

Miles and miles of this sameness lie before us with much expectation about getting to the Platte. I wonder about this word, "Platte," as I have never heard it used before.

Our first day out on the road, when we stop, it is for the night. We make our fires. Put up our tents, while Momma prepares the food. We are happy to be sitting still while we eat supper. The dishes are cleaned. Then to sleep. For me, it will be the best part of the day.

This evening as we camp, I feel emboldened. I ask Mister Jason to explain this word, "Platte," to me as I think he might know. Doing this small gesture puts me in mind of the days when we children were crowded in Mistress's rooms, and she would read to us. There would sometimes be questions that required an explanation of some of the stories she read.

"The Platte is a very long river," he begins. "Very long. I do not know how long, but it could stretch out in the hundreds of miles. It was first named by the French explorers. 'Platte' is a French word that means 'flat river.'

"It twists and turns for all of these miles and miles. There is a north end and a south end. Mister Cooper tells me we will cross and recross it many times. In some places it is deep, and in others shallow."

Mister Jason's explanation of the Platte sounds like something of a great tale. It reminds me of how much I miss hearing stories told. Then I realize, in truth, it is as if I am inside the story—a great adventure story told of a journey on the Overland Trail to California—only it is my story, Hope's Journey.

* * *

We stop five miles below Fort Leavenworth to repair a supply pump for removing water. Mister Cooper carries it with him for a friend who is already at the mining town in California. We will stop here for the night.

"Those are Delaware people," Mister Walter says to Momma and me as he sees them coming toward us. An older woman, like a grandmother; a younger woman, like a mother; and a young boy come up to us.

"They seem so sweet and gentle," Momma says. Mister Walter smiles. I am glad he stands nearby.

"I do not see how they mean us harm," Momma adds. The women are dressed in soft, loose-fitting brown clothing made from animal skin. It is fringed on the bottom edges.

"Deerskin," Momma says.

The people wear ornaments of bone and shell on their wrists and ankles. The grandmother wears a deer hide shawl decorated with beading, which hangs over her shoulders, and turkey feathers are attached. Their shoes, moccasins, are made of the same brown deerskin, lined with a soft fur and decorated with beading. They are beautiful to behold.

"They are only tired and hungry," Momma says.

The little boy speaks English, and he tells me they walked most of the night to get here. Momma offers them food. They sit with us and eat. The boy tells us they are farming people. "It is our mothers and grandmothers who do most of the farming," the boy says. "They grow and harvest all the food we eat—corn, squash, and beans. The men in our village hunt all the meat—deer, elk, and turkey—and catch fish in the rivers." We sit and eat in quiet.

Then the mother speaks to the older woman. The grandmother talks to the little boy. He listens and takes something from inside a parcel they carry. He hands Momma two brown and thickish dried-out round disks. They look something like rocks of dirt. Momma smiles and thanks them.

"Grandmother tells me to say this to you: Find these on the road. Pick them up and keep them. When there is no wood, use them to build the cooking fire. They will help to build a hot fire. You will need hot fires where you are going."

Momma smiles again and thanks the boy and his grandmother and mother. There are many reasons, besides cooking our food, out in these wide-open spaces to keep the fires burning hot. For light. And to warm ourselves in the cold nights. And to dry our clothes when we wash them or have to swim across the water. Also, to keep away wild animals. It is important to have for survival. We are grateful for this great gift.

The grandmother thanks us again. I think we all

are grateful for what each has given the other. They stand and start on their way.

"I see you have already begun to learn the ways of this wilderness," Mister Cooper says.

The next day, we continue to travel up along the river. Sometimes the waters are shallow enough to wade through. Other times the waters are deep and moving and require that we ferry the wagons across or swim the horses. A boy who is the age of Edward, one of Mister Jason's younger brothers, probably the age of fourteen or fifteen, thought he saw one of his family's horses in distress. Kindly he jumped in to offer help or swim the horse to the other side. The boy jumped into the water, but he did not appear again from the water's depth. The horse did.

We could not move on. The boy's father and some of the other men searched for him, but he was never found. By nightfall, all wagons finally were able to get across the water. This night, there is much sadness. We could all hear the tears and wailing cries of his mother.

The next day, we move on.

Momma says the lack of home comforts adds to the worry and talk of sickness. Everyday ailments— aches and pains such as headaches, toothaches, and muscle aches—seem much worse. Constant talk and worry of sickness and disease such as cholera and pneumonia do not ease the mind. Sometimes when Mister Jason complains of headache, Momma gives him a concoction of a small amount of brandy mixed with something else. It does seem to revive him. When others complain of sickness, she helps where she can. As we walk, Momma scouts for plants—tree bark, herbs she knows are useful in cooking or for her medicine cures, and the dirt rocks.

As we walk today, I cannot understand the look on Poppa's face. For many there is great weariness that is not eased through the night. There will be many more rivers to cross.

The sky here in this wilderness land is most changeable. This morning we awake with the wind blowing violently. The thunder claps loud and hard overhead when there is nothing but the sky as a covering. The rain is cold and raw. We keep marching on. Up ahead in the distance, we can see that the rain has stopped, and the weather is clear. If we keep moving, soon we will move out of this storm. We will not be able to stop to dry out until evening when we camp. Then we will make a warm fire and have our meal before we sleep.

We have reached our destination for the night. This day we made sixteen miles. When we stop and camp, Mister Jason and Poppa, as well as some of the other men, set off to hunt. They return with turkeys, prairie hens, and ducks. We are grateful for our good fortune. As night sets in, there are good cooking smells in the air. The music and singing about our "Home Sweet Home" starts. I find this routine most enjoyable. With so many miles ahead, this song offers comfort. I like the words:

"Be it ever so humble,
There is no place like home."

I sing these words along with the refrain and my mind will not let me stop wondering. *Home,* it says to me. *Where is our home?* Now that we are on the adventure journey, where is the home for Momma, Poppa, and me? The people on this trail are going to a new home. Somehow these words to this song make me feel sad. I roll up in my blanket. I do not want Momma or Poppa to know that I am sad enough to cry after such a happy day, and I must make my happiness last.

We travel over plains and roads that rise and fall. There are those that are hot and dry, and sometimes we come to and cross small streams. Some of them have pretty names. Days ago, we passed the Little

Blue River, a large muddy creek. We camped there. The teams of animals could drink, some people swam and bathed. Some people caught fish.

The road is hard. Though there are places the land is covered with beautiful flowers and good pastures for grazing, we must not linger too long. We continue our march. There are other companies on this road ahead of us and behind us. Even on these trails, the crowds do not go away. We must push and move forward. No matter about exhaustion. We have to keep going. Moving or stopping or packing or unpacking, we have to be readying or ready to move.

I am happy for the times when there are good grasses for the animals to graze. We let them go so they can wander and feed and rest. Eating the cayenne pepper Momma adds to the food causes me to sweat.

"We are only miles from Fort Kearny," Mister Cooper says as he moves up and down the row of wagons. He hopes we can continue to make twenty miles each day. I suppose he is telling us this to give us confidence that a destination is soon in sight. There is nothing behind us to see from where we have come. There has to be something up ahead to look forward to other than miles and miles of wilderness and more of the same.

There was a dreadful storm last night—wind and rain and hail. There was sharp lightning that killed two oxen. I am happy all our animals are safe. The wind was so high, I thought it might take the cover from the wagon. I found myself feeling sad about the animals that died.

"It is terrible about the killed animals," Momma said. "But it is also a good thing—now we have fresh meat." When the men hunt for animals or fish in the lakes, all the food is shared.

Fort Kearny is on the riverbank of the Platte. We are told it is a place that soothes the soul of the weary traveler. There we will find houses with walls, ceilings, and floors. Supplies can be purchased. Animals can be reshoed.

When we camp this night, we are told the next fort after Fort Kearny is Fort Laramie. The way west of that fort, cholera is not so much a problem. I think we all long for this place, however far it may be. I cannot let myself think of numbers and miles. I simply must continue to plant one foot in front of the other and just keep marching as the days blend together.

Now we come to another small creek. The banks are steep and muddy, and where we cross has to be filled with brush to keep the cattle from sinking into the mud. It seems to take forever and a day, but Momma says, "Do not think that way. Think only of what you are doing at the time you are doing it."

Finally, it is 6:00 p.m. That is all that matters. I am glad for the call to make camp. Tomorrow will come soon enough, and when it does, it will just be more of the same. Cold nights. Hot days. Wind. Rain. Thunder. Poppa does what he can to stay close to Mister Jason to keep him safe. It is like this every day. There is nothing to do but keep myself moving.

My mind thinks on what we encountered on this road today. We passed seven graves. I feel sad that I am counting them. Counting these deaths and what remains of someone's hopes and dreams that never happened. Mister Cooper has said there will be many more. He tells us some are buried right under the same road we are traveling upon. People have done this so that the earth becomes packed down tight around their loved ones. This prevents the wild beasts of the plains—coyotes and wolves—from digging up the remains to devour them. I am so glad that up to now, we have only heard them. We have not seen many of them on this way.

"Take care of yourselves! Make sure you will not end up in such a way," Mister Cooper says. He is happy we made twenty-two miles this day before we camp. As I climb into my warm blanket on this cold night, I am grateful for my name. *Which name?* I say to myself. *Clementine?* I ask my mind. *Oh no*, it answers back. *Though the word has a nice sound to it, you have never been a Clementine. You have always been filled with Hope.*

Tonight, as we camp, I think today is a day I saw an elephant. We saw buffalo for the first time. It is such a large beast, like the oxen, but they seem so much bigger with their large, deep shoulders and humped heads and necks. The hair on the head is long and shorter on the body. They run with their heads help up, bravely looking forward. Mister Bristle, one traveler on this train, took aim and shot. The noise caused the herd to turn. The herd dashed off. I was grateful they did not stampede in our direction. I was sad for the animal but glad that we have fresh meat and what foods it can provide.

We move on and on. In days that are too many to count, we have a bright clear morning. The wind blows strong. We arrive at a little creek called Big Blue River. Here is the first sign of anything green for a long time. We camp here for the night.

In more days' time, we come upon a group of traveling men from Fort Kearny. They tell us they have seen the elephant at that place. We pass so many more graves along the way. Soon we will be out of grass and the extra feed we bought for the animals.

It is what we will use as we get closer to our destination point, where we can buy more supplies.

Today, we reach a pretty place. It is Fort Kearny. It is like seeing the elephant, but I am not so sure this is what is meant by that remark. It is beautiful and has "all the comforts of home," someone says.

There are fourteen houses. Three of the buildings are framed, and there are houses made of sod, or mud. Poppa tells me, "These houses have roofs made of dry grass." There is a store to purchase supplies, a blacksmith shop, a hospital, a post office, and rooms to rent. Mister Jason goes to the post office to mail a letter home to Mistress.

Someone who lives and works at the fort says 3,200 wagons passed before us and three hundred more are in the vicinity, nearby. Again, everything in this journey is described by numbers. I have never thought of things on such a grand scale.

We let the animals walk freely and feed on the grass. We make camp on the bank of the Platte. Mister Jason will rent a room for himself this night, where he can have a warm bath.

Someone yells, "Remember the Sabbath!" Then I think this must be the Sunday day of the week. A preacher calls all those willing to come hear words of the Bible.

"Let us pray," he says. I do. My only words are of gratefulness for having come safely along this way with Momma and Poppa.

This morning, we got an earlier start. At 4:00 a.m. we had our breakfast, struck the tents, and we were on our way again. Our next destination stop is Fort Laramie, more than three hundred miles away. Our food supplies must last until then.

CHAPTER SIX

New Ways of Cooking and Eating

As we walk this morning, I think back on the things that brought us here and I remember. Back at Belle Hills, the day after Mister Jason shared news of his decision to travel west to the gold fields, he had come to Mistress's rooms. When I arrived there that morning to help prepare her for the day, he greeted me. "Clementine, your mistress and I have something to discuss with you." My heart felt heavy in my chest.

"Sit down, Clementine," Mistress began softly. And then she inquired if I had slept well and had my breakfast.

"Yes, mam," I said, but I did not know why she would ask me this.

"Mister Jason must rely on you on this trip too," she continued. "There is much planning and not much time. You must help with the food preparations and the supplies."

"Yes, Mistress, I will," I said.

"Good," Mister Jason added. "You must read and study Mister Hastings's book, *The Emigrant's Guide*."

At once a feeling of sickness and dread came over me. I was glad to be already sitting down.

"You mean the awful book . . . that caused the deaths of the poor families?" Looking toward my mistress, I put my hand to my mouth, horrified I said these words aloud.

"Yes. That one. But not all of the book is awful," Mister Jason said. "My captain assures us some portions of the guide are trustworthy." He motioned it toward me. It was not such a big book, but it felt heavy in my hands. "You must help Adelaide study those parts of the guide so that she knows what cooking utensils to use and how to pack things within the wagon. As the cook, she must know which food preparations are best for the journey and what is to be carried within the supplies, and she must pay special attention to storage to keep the food from spoiling in such harsh conditions."

Now as I walk along, I recall the day when I was told to study the Hastings guide. In my mind, it is not a very good one. He said nothing about building fires with fuel found along the way. It causes me to wonder what other things are missing.

I remember that one evening as I was reading to Momma, Mistress came into the kitchen.

"You will be good help to Mister Jason and this family," Mistress said to me. I remember looking up to smile at her, but she had already turned to walk away.

"All of the food and everything we have must be fit and carried inside the wagon for the long journey," I said to Momma after Mistress left. "We must have enough to last until we reach a supply spot where we can buy more. We must have enough food to last."

Momma smiled at me. "I am used to this. This is no different than before I came to work in the kitchen here at Belle Hills Farm. We had to make the food allotment last until the next one. That's why I always kept a garden."

Still, this worried me. There was no place for a garden to grow along the trail. I thought about the poor families who perished. I never told her about those unfortunate people.

"What do they say about the flour?" Momma asked me. I read this section to her.

As I think back to what I read to Momma, there was no mention of flour other than how much to bring for each person. While we were in St. Louis, when Mister Jason was healing from cholera, he gave Momma the advertisement he found in the newspaper for a special kind of flour best used on the open trail. It is said to be treated in a kiln, a very hot oven. This is what keeps the flour sweet and good and prevents it from souring like other flours, the notice said. I reckon the flour to be very important to him as well as Momma. Over his life, he has grown very fond of Momma's biscuits.

Momma had said she figured supplies and food must be stored so they take up as little space as possible inside the wagon and kept safe and packed in lidded cans and barrels.

"It's probably different than what we do inside of Belle Hills, but still everything must be secure," she had said. I see how things happened together to help us journey well.

Momma used strong double cotton sacks and barrels and boxes. Bacon, a necessary food, must be stored and placed in a box and surrounded by bran to keep the fat from melting away. It should be placed in the bottom of the wagon, which is the coolest place on the trail. Butter can be preserved by first boiling it, then skimming the "scum" off the top as it rises and keeping the clear part. This too must be stored in an airtight tin.

Out here on these plains it is recommended for each person's food allotment to be: two hundred pounds of flour, one hundred pounds of bacon, ten pounds of rice, five pounds of coffee, two pounds of tea, twenty-five pounds of sugar, one-half bushel of dried beans, one bushel of dried fruit such as apples and peaches, two pounds of saleratus for baking, ten pounds of salt, one-half bushel of cornmeal, two gallons of vinegar, and two gallons of molasses.

Momma also brought black currants and chili peppers for seasoning. She keeps barrels of pickling liquid to make pickled bell peppers, pickled lemons, or pickled cabbage when we can find them. Daily, she gives us a helping of something that is pickled. She said it will keep us from getting certain diseases that can cause you to grow weak and bleed about your gums.

In Momma's medicine crate is a good supply of whiskey and brandy. Back home Mister Uncle would only drink of these after eating Momma's evening supper meals. Some people on the wagon train drink these spirits as a pastime after the day ends. Mister Cooper allows it at no other time, but not too much of it at any one time is allowed.

Food is cooked on an open fire. Momma says until she got to understand it, cooking in this way for her was an awful job. "I did cook this way as a child, when I was home with my mother," she says. This causes her to think and remember her mother, my grandmother, someone I will never know. From her mother, she learned to collect kindling wood to build a good fire. But here on the plains there is not always much wood. The grandmother of the Delaware tribe was right—making a cooking fire is best done with the buffalo chips we have found.

"I see your cook is making good use of the ways of the wilderness," Mister Walter tells Mister Jason when he discovers Momma using them to fuel our cooking fires. This is something more that causes me to wonder what Mistress would think about this. I know now where these soft brown rocks come from—what they are.

I never thought so much about food and numbers before this journey. Everything now is talked of less in words and more in numbers. What day is this? How many more days? How many miles have we gone today? How many more shall we go tomorrow? How much flour do we need? How many oxen? How many more pounds of flour is left? We must not run out of supplies and food. Yet the farther away we travel from Missouri, the higher the prices are each time we stop to resupply.

At our last supply and stopping point Mister Jason was able to buy the tins of oysters Momma loves. Back home in Virginia, we ate them regularly, being so close to the Chesapeake Bay. Momma was so happy to receive the little tin. It made for a nice change from our usual meal of bacon and bread.

Out here on these wide-open plains, I think about the unfortunate people lost in the mountains with nothing to eat. I think how miserable it must be to run out of food. And how we must have enough so that it lasts. I tell my wandering mind to stop these thoughts. But I cannot.

We all worry about shortage of food and

supplies—not just food for us but also grain for the animals. It must be kept in airtight containers. The animals will eat the old grass in the spring, but it does not hold in this climate. This job of food is a big part of our adventure journey.

And most important is water. Running out of fresh water is a very big concern. We must be careful up ahead of some places along the river where it is not fit to drink. We all become knowledgeable of it. Poppa shows me what to look for. We look around the water's edges. If there are places that are white and gritty, it is probably salt making it alkaline. Drinking small amounts of it is not harmful to people, but it is terribly poisonous to the animals. Their stomachs cannot digest it. If the animals drink the bad water, they suffer a horrible death. Sometimes the grass can be a yellowish-reddish color. It is another sign. Animals must never be allowed near it.

Bread is our mainstay. It is eaten at every meal. Breakfast each day is bread with butter or bacon and strong black coffee. If we do not have butter, we use lard. If we are out of lard, we use buffalo fat if we have it. At each place we stop, we are sure to resupply certain items such as bacon. We get bread with a piece of bacon hot out of Momma's cast-iron skillet. When there is nothing else to eat, there is bread. Momma cooks it daily over the open fire using the fuel given to her by the grandmother and her family.

When she can find them, Momma picks acorns along the way. When there is enough, she removes the cap and uses the oak nut. These little things are pounded into flour. Then she mixes the acorn flour and water together and fries it in bacon grease. This food she calls acorn flapjacks. It is very good tasting. This is something she remembers of her life with my grandmother.

One morning Momma mixes the flapjack batter with dried fruit she has softened by boiling it. Then she fries the flapjacks in her cast-iron skillet with grease. It is so close to the taste of Momma's plum pudding. At suppertime we are all happy to sit still. It is the best part of the day, along with Momma's cooking. So much daily walking makes the hunger so great. It is always good to be food satisfied. This night, I think of home. I sing myself to sleep . . . *there's no place like home.* But, before I close my eyes, a thought comes to me. Being so close with Momma and Poppa is home enough for me.

As the newspaper suggested, Momma prepares and keeps on hand a food called pilot bread. It is made from flour and water with no grease. It is baked for a very long time until it is very dry. The pilot bread is dried out so that it lasts. On rainy days we eat it by dipping it in strong black coffee. Sometimes it is the only thing to eat. Back in St. Louis, it was one of the ready-made breads and crackers advertised to be sold as "prepared especially for *the California and Oregon Emigrants.*" Momma says she just prefers to cook her own.

There is still talk of cholera and other concerns floating through the air. More gossip and worry glide along on the wind. When we camp, Mister Walter speaks to Mister Jason.

"Before the white man set foot here, this was the land of Sioux, Cherokee, Blackfoot, and others," Mister Walter says. "As more and more emigrants from the east and other places in the world came here to these plains, they took up all the space. Those people are being driven out."

"You seem to know a good deal about this," Mister Jason replies.

"I ought to. My momma's mother—my grandmother—was Sioux."

Hearing these words from Mister Walter makes me think about *my* home and how easily it can be taken away. We on this wagon train are traveling through someone else's home. It makes me continue to wonder: Where is *our* home now? Momma's, Poppa's, and mine.

For now, I tell myself home on this road is our wagon. I look at Poppa cleaning the dust out of the tight spaces of the wheels. Momma is airing out the wagon—tending to the things inside the wagon, making sure everything is packed and ready as it should be when we move again. She tightens the ropes of the bonnet. It must be kept tied—closed tightly to keep out the dust. Watching Momma and Poppa tend their chores to prepare to continue our journey takes away some of the sad memory of leaving Belle Hills behind. My mind tells my heart, for now, remember, being with them must be home enough.

There does not seem any need to hurry. It will be time to go soon. There is no dust now. The air is clear. Still, each wagon is being readied and spread out so the one behind does not choke on the gritty powder that rises as we walk. We are very far west of Independence now. I can see far in the distance from where we have come. Across the prairie the wind blows moving the grass from side to side like it is dancing.

As we begin our walk, the white tops of the wagons come into view. This place with all its worries and fears has a strange beauty. Soon enough as the sun heats the day, the air will change. It will become dry, and dust and clouds of mosquitoes will form. Momma tells me to put grease on my lips to keep them from drying out from the wind and sun. And to keep my arms covered and away from biting bugs. She gives us some of the peppermint leaves to rub on our skin. Mosquitoes and other insects do not like its smell. But still when they bite, it is misery.

When we have completed this day's travel, it is time to sleep, my mind says to my heart. *Yes, for now this is your home, with all of its strangeness.*

Today we come across a stretch of bleached skeletons of the buffalo strewn across the plains. Traveling many more miles, we come to a spring of cold water. When we camp this day, we see a tribe. Mister Jason says they are the Sioux people. I think of Mister Walter and his grandmother.

Though this brings up much worry and tensions are high in our company, we pass the tribe peacefully. I wonder if they are as curious about us as I am about them. I wonder what these people, the Sioux, think of this parade of emigrants. And where are we all going. I wonder if they are fearful of us and the thousands of wagons and even more emigrants to come.

Without warning, a voice from up ahead of the train yells, "Buffalo," again and again. Then, everything halts. Everyone gets quiet. Everything, wheels, hooves, and feet, stops. It seems as though the wind all comes to a stop at the same moment at the mention of the word. I look ahead. I do not see anything. But as I stare hard at the horizon, what is in front of me seems to be getting bigger and moving closer toward me. Then I feel a trembling and shaking motion of the earth under my feet. It grows as big and loud as the puffing steam locomotive we rode so many days ago. And then I see them . . . so many.

They come toward us from the front. There is nothing we can do to get out of their way. They run fast.

I stare because I cannot make sense of what I see—a line of dark, heavy clouds hover just above the ground. Everyone shouts and rushes around. Some of the men get off their horses and wave their hats and arms over their heads. We women join in, waving our arms and bonnets, too. Some gather pots and pans—spoons or sticks from the ground, anything we can get our hands on that will make noise. One emigrant takes out his trumpet and begins blasting sounds. He makes it scream and honk. We holler and yelp and jump up and down—anything we can do to keep the buffalo from coming through our camp.

Mister Cooper has Mister Walter take three men with him to hitch a pair of mules to a lightweight wagon to follow the herd for the purpose of killing a buffalo. They bring the meat back to camp and hand out portions. Some people do not want this, but Momma takes a portion and packs it in salt so that she can prepare it for eating when we camp again, as well as the buffalo fat. Mister Walter says adding the fat to the meat gives it more flavor.

Momma is excited to know the taste of buffalo meat from a preparation of a food known as pemmican that Mister Walter shares with her. Momma spoke with Mister Walter many times about this until she memorized the way to make it.

To make pemmican, first you cut buffalo meat thin into strips. Then you hang it up to dry in the sun or before a hot fire. After it has dried, you pound it between two stones to reduce it to a powder. Place this powder into a bag of the animal's hide, with the hair on the outside. Melt some of the buffalo fat. Then you pour that into the bag. Sew up the bag. The pemmican can be eaten raw, and many prefer it this way. It can also be mixed with a little flour and boiled. It is a very wholesome and nutritious food. It will keep fresh for a long time.

As we continue the move west, there are stretches of the trail where the air and the sky and the heavens are so clear, as clear as window glass. The wind blows cool and pure and so sweet. We come across many different shapes of rock. There is hardly any greenery here. These rock formations decorate the landscapes as back home did the trees and flowers and fields and gardens. There are signposts and landmarks along the way that mark the trail to give the heart hope and joy that you know you are on the right path. These places have much beauty and majesty. It is as if my eye cannot look at these rock figures long enough to feel a true satisfaction. Passing by them leaves the eye wanting to see them more. These sites inspire my heart as I move in these wide-open spaces. So far, I think, for me, every step of this part of our journey is seeing more of the elephant.

The land we come to here is not level. We are on the Lower Platte. The soil is sandy, and wood is scarce, but the weather is fair and beautiful. We start earlier this morning than we did on other days. We pass through a place called Ash Hollow. It is a deep, narrow valley with a river rushing through it. It was given this name because of the red ash trees that are found here. We have to use ropes to ease the wagons down the steep hills. Here we finally have a good supply of firewood and water.

From Ash Hollow we travel three miles or so and come to a place called Quicksand Creek. It is bad to cross because of the quicksand. This is a strange piece of the ground. It is most of all sandy—not a solid ground—and is difficult to walk on. The loose soil can pull you under it. Do not walk on this ground when you are alone.

After five miles or so, we come to the foot of Castle Bluffs south of the river and camp. These cliffs rise up to several hundred feet, Mister Walter says. They have weathered many storms over the years of their existence. From a distance, they appear as ancient, ruined castles like the ones I imagined in the stories Mistress would read. Wherever we walk over the days and days, the road is dry and sandy. The biting mosquitoes are most unkind.

After many miles, we come across a village of Sioux. They call their homes lodges. They are made of tanned buffalo skins. The buffalo means life to these people living in this wilderness. Every part of the animal is important to them for their lives. The buffalo meat is used for food. From the skin, they make dwellings and clothing. It is also used to construct the walls of their lodges. Their tools and some of the decorations they wear are made from the bone. The women wear dresses made of tanned buffalo skin. The dresses are decorated with many beads. As we come closer to their village, we are beckoned to stop. Some of the adventurers in our wagon train want to camp here in order to trade and barter with the Sioux. Mister Walter is happy for this as they represent family to him.

We make camp this night nearby their village. During the evening meal, two of the men come to our campfire. They motion to talk with Poppa. Mister Walter explains to us the reason for their visit.

"They have never seen a Black man before," Mister

Walter says. "To them, Ezekiel is *Big Medicine*—someone with special spiritual powers. After a long and big battle, only the one bravest and the strongest of the warriors on the field is honored. That is the only man who has the right to paint his skin black, with the coal from the war fire. When he is given this right and privilege, everyone knows him to be the greatest warrior—the man of power who has been touched by God, the Creator."

Then when the talking is over, they each offer their hand for Poppa to shake.

"That does explain something," Poppa chuckles. "Those two fellows came up to me earlier on the trail. I greeted them both with a smile. Then one took my arm in his hand, licked his fingers, and started rubbing my skin. I guess they were trying to see if it would rub off."

Later I hear Poppa chuckle and say to himself, "Big Medicine." Then Poppa's hearty laugh follows. It is good to hear your poppa laugh so during such a trail as this.

During this new day, we approach a formation of rock known as Courthouse Rock. Its broad bottom is miles wide. Mister Walter calls it one of the many famous guiding landmarks we will see as we make our way. Travelers look for these signs to let them know they are on the right path.

About twenty-two miles later we come to a crossing at Smith's Creek. Smith's Creek is the most beautiful stream we have found since leaving Missouri. The river flows from the hills over a clear, sandy bed. The water is cool and delicious in my dry and parched mouth. I must say it is a nice change from drinking the muddiness of the waters of the Platte.

We pass many low places with water that we are unable to drink. As we come upon Courthouse Rock, it appears much closer than it really is. Some men from our camp decide to walk there, but they return before long, not having completed their task. "It is much farther away than you think!" they tell us when they return to camp.

It is a circular rock that stands on a little ridge. It is so named, as many say it resembles a courthouse or jailhouse.

As we get upon the guidepost, we see words scrawled across a ledge. They read "Post Office." The words are cut into the rock. Under the sign are cavities or gashes in the stone that were caused by weather, time, and water. In one of these holes is a number of letters that have been crammed in there by those adventurers who have already passed by this spot. Mister Walter says they were left here for their friends who are somewhere behind them.

This is one of the ways the emigrants on this trail

talk and give news to those who may be in different wagon trains. Another way is to write notes on sun-bleached buffalo skulls or shoulder blades. Often, we come across the bones—all that is left of these great animals—strewn across the landscape, drying out in the sun.

We pass many of these "note bones" along parts of the road. There are other ways people on the trail talk to one another. We often come upon a stick that is jammed upright into the ground on the side of the trail. At the top of the stick, a slit has been made. There, a note has been placed, wedged between the cut, waiting for its reader.

The day after we come upon another guiding landmark sight, known as Chimney Rock. It is a most unusual shape for a rock—a pillar that looks like a chimney without its house attached. It is at least three hundred feet high. Emigrants along the trail engrave their names into the soft stone. As soon as we start to camp, the clouds begin to darken and thicken. It gives the sky an angry appearance. Living and walking out in this wilderness, you begin to learn the good and bad weather signs. The signs say the storm will be violent.

In an hour or so, rain begins to pour down and terrible winds blow.

Thankfully, we have enough time before the storm

comes upon us. We lock all the wheels of the wagons so they will not blow away. Then we are instructed how to tend the cattle and livestock to keep them from stampeding. And thankfully again, the storm leaves as quickly as it came.

As the winds sweep the sky clear of clouds, the moon and stars shine brightly. I declare, the nature of this wilderness country is a most beautiful picture and all at once surprising.

There is plenty of good grazing for the animals. But as we travel, we are troubled by buffalo gnats. These are more of a nuisance than the Virginia gnats back home. These cousins are much, much bigger. We beat and swipe the air around us to try to keep them away. I hope we can easily pass through this buzzy cloud, leaving them behind.

Finally, after twenty miles or so, we arrive at Scotts Bluff. It is named for a trader who has traveled through this area many times. We are all happy that our cattle and livestock are lucky to have so much sweet grass to graze.

There is a small trading post on the trail at Scotts Bluff. It is run by a husband and a wife. He is a black-smith and there are some supplies he keeps for the travelers. This is also a place to be in touch with others on the road. Inside, emigrants have covered the walls

with letters and notes written to their friends and loved ones.

During the next day's travel, we go up a deep valley for a number of miles after we reach the highest height of the bluffs. From this view, we can see Laramie's snow-covered peak.

We move downhill, over barren country. It is broken with deep gaps in the road and places where it is very wet. Some of the places are hollowed out by wind and water. At nooning time when we break for midday meal, we find poor grass and no water.

Some miles back, a man on our train accidently shot himself with his own pistol. Since that time, he has not shown much improvement to healing the wound in his arm. His arm may need to be taken off to save his life.

When we break for camp, Momma uses the buffalo chips we collected for the fire to cook our supper. Each day passes into another and another. It is hard to tell one day from the next. At Belle Hills each chore told the day of the week. Here chores have no order—all has to do with when we can stop. On days when we halt long enough, Momma checks supplies and airs out the wagon. When we come near water, we hope it is clear enough of muddiness to drink and wash the clothes.

The next morning is more of the same, but a

happiness dwells in me now. I think of how far we've come. We still have a long way to go, but we're now closer to our destination point than we are to St. Louis, Missouri, and Alexandria, Virginia.

We come to a harsh sight—many wagons abandoned and destroyed. When I say my prayers this night, I will remember to pray this will not happen to us.

Tonight, when we camp on the bank of the North Fork of the Platte, Mister Cooper tells us we are only five miles from Fort Laramie. This day, we went twenty-two miles. At this fort we can rest and resupply and do cleaning chores.

The morning opens into newness with a clear sky. It already has a pleasant feel to it. We guzzle our hot coffee and morning bread, and we are off on the trail by 4:00 a.m. We travel over a hilly road before coming to a running stream of muddy water.

"It is the Laramie River," Mister Cooper tells us. It is about one hundred yards wide. We cross it with our teams. The water comes up to the axles of our wheels. To see Fort Laramie in the distance is a very welcome sight. The Black Hills and Laramie Peak stand behind. It leaves a pretty picture in my mind. This day, we stop at noon. There is little grass for the animals to graze. Many wagon train companies have already come ahead of us. Still, it is a good resting place. We have seen many elephants on this way.

Fort Laramie is a military post. It stands within a valley. We meet many others bound for California. Here there are twenty houses enclosed within a thick wall. Momma tells Mister Jason what supplies we need. After so many days and nights of wide-open spaces and rocks, it is beautiful to look at while we rest.

Momma tells me today we are nearly out of the month of June now. Mister Cooper tells us soon enough we will arrive at Independence Rock. *Independence Rock,* I say to myself, and I think of my poet-friend, Miss Phillis Wheatley. What would she think of me arriving soon at a place called Independence Rock? This causes happiness inside me.

CHAPTER SEVEN

Much Beauty along the Trail

July 1, 1849, to July 27, 1849
Fort Laramie to South Pass

As we travel farther west of Fort Laramie, the land changes quickly. The trail of the North Platte becomes rough and rocky country. We move along a steep ridge, a narrow mountain range. We cross many streams. There is fresh water and grass. We can smell the fragrance of pine and juniper in the air before we come to the trees. The narrow waterways run through the canyon. Mister Cooper reminds us that though this part of our journey will have its hardships and worries, as we continue to move west of the fort, there will be no talk or worry of cholera.

At this part of the trail, there is very little to no firewood fuel. We must rely on buffalo chips. In the high places of the Black Hills, where there are no buffalo, we use only scrub timber. Mister Walter says a few more miles farther west we will find sage and greasewood. He tells Momma, "Greasewood is a woody shrub that grows wild in these dry places." He says it is used for fire fuel and can be used to help digestion, as well as made into a poultice, a mash, to spread on aches and pains as well as bruises. I declare I like its smell—a mixture of scents such as pine, lemon, and some of Momma's spices.

Sometimes we come to pieces of wood strewn on

the path that were once parts of wagons. We use these abandoned and broken bits for fuel. We also find other broken wooden things such as boxes, crates, and barrels that have been left behind. Though so much of the travel is easier, the roads seem longer and much harder. These paths are rocky. The rocks can cut and bruise the animals' legs and hooves. At stopping time, Poppa applies the greasewood mash to the sore places on the animals' legs.

Mistress was right in her uneasiness and concern for Mister Jason. On this journey I hold worry for us all. There are still many perils, seen as well as unseen. This trail holds many hard death experiences because we are surrounded by a vast wilderness. What is worse are the unknown risks of disease. Farther out along the way there are fewer and fewer remedy cures. There are animal deaths as well as human deaths, and these many different kinds of deaths take a toll on us all. Nerves are frayed. Heads and hearts are weary. With so much more of the road to go, all we can do is continue to move ahead and pray for our safe arrival.

We learn that a man in our wagon train has died. He suffered his injury during the buffalo stampede. He was doing his part to steer the beasts away from camp. He may have been paying close attention to the movement of the herd when one beast snuck up on him. That animal gored the man with its horn and ended his life.

At this point on the trail, Mister Cooper speaks to us.

"This trail . . . ," Mister Cooper begins as we stand around the hole in the ground where we would bury the man who was gored. Mr. Cooper pauses to take a breath. "This trail—it takes getting used to. Though you never really do, do you?" Mister Jason says Mister Cooper takes this death particularly hard. He knew this man well.

As horrible as any death is, this too, I think, is what is meant by "seeing the elephant." On a journey such as this, there is much that is lost, and yet I must believe there is so much more to be found. The human self has to decide what is the gain. Or if it is worth the gain. Is it a prize enough to keep moving forward? I say yes.

As we travel today, I cannot help but think and worry about the poor animals. To move as we do, they must be driven and pushed so much harder than the trail pushes us—especially the mules. Sometimes water is not found immediately. If enough water has not been gathered for the next part of the journey, the animal may stop and will not move until water is provided for them. Still, they must be driven on until good, clean water can be found. Some are not strong enough. Some are failing and fast. Poppa was right to purchase these animals we have. The majority of our mules are one to two years of age. Poppa said for the life of these beasts, this is a fit age for a journey such as this.

As we travel, Mister Cooper stops the wagons to give the animals a rest. This land is not kind. Some are pushed too hard. When an animal has had enough, it will drop down to its knees in its harness, exhausted, and go no farther. Lately, we see more animal carcasses as we cross this pass than any other time, too many for me to count.

We come across a wagon train whose mules are nearly worn down and not able to draw their wagons farther. Those people, emigrants from the country of Sweden, are constructing pack saddles, hoping to get farther along the trail. They have abandoned all their wagons and much valuable property. But there is no other way. Daily along the trail we see wagons left together with their chains, bars, and various utensils that are worth picking up. But we do not.

"It is another kind of a hard road to carry around someone else's misery," Momma says as we pass by the remains of a wagon train.

Some emigrants we meet along the way say they have never seen Negroes before. As far back as St. Louis, a woman in our wagon train company said this

to Momma and me as we sat waiting for Poppa and Mister Jason to conduct their business of purchasing supplies.

"I have never seen a Negro before. I wonder how you could ever be like us," the woman said, coming so close to us, upon seeing Momma and me. The woman had three children clinging to her skirt and held one child in her arms. Momma looked at the infant she carried.

"Is your child faring well?" Momma asked gently. "I'd take a look at him if you will allow me." But the woman's husband appeared and ushered her and his children away from us. We did not see the family again much as they were in a farther part of the wagon train than where we were. Momma, Poppa, and I keep to ourselves as much as possible.

As we move farther and farther west, we come to the river crossing. There is a good amount of green grass for grazing the horses, mules, and cattle. I am happy for them—these poor beasts. They eat heartily. In the whole of the wagon train, we only lose one mule getting across the river due to drowning.

We have to travel all night at times. On one occasion we make camp after dark. It is a moonless night. We stop because we can go no farther without rest. There is a terrible stench in the air. All night long I think it is something passing on the breeze. It causes a most fitful sleep. I feel my stomach churning, though I had little to nothing at the evening meal. I think I should ask Momma for a remedy. The early morning light finds our wagon company camped close between two dead oxen. There is a dead ox on each side of our wagon and one horse as well. We have to move fast before breakfast. I do not think I can ever eat breakfast again. The heat of the air and the stench of the rotting carcasses are difficult for me to bear. There is a sweet, sharp foulness about it. The smell fills up in my head and lingers there.

On and on we journey, averaging fifteen to twenty miles a day over cactus, sagebrush, and hot sands. Walking so much, the one pair of shoes I was equipped with gives out. I tie them to my feet with rope wrapped around the bottom. Mister Jason says at our next supply stop I can have a pair of boots.

We come to meet a group of Pawnee. They are farming people. They are used to trading with Fort Laramie and emigrants as they pass by. This place we are walking was once their land. By now, Momma has no fear of speaking easily with these people we meet. Our contacts with the people of this land are friendly and useful. Momma barters with one of the women in the group. A cast-iron skillet for a pair of moccasins for me.

"I have become so accustomed to cooking out on an open fire. I find I use few of the cooking utensils I brought along for it. One cast-iron skillet is enough for most meals, plus, it helps to lighten our load," she tells me.

The moccasins are so soft and comfortable. They almost seem too beautiful to wear on such rugged ground. They are well suited. There are blue and red beads around the top and front of the foot. Sometimes walking along, I let my mind wander to think of returning to Belle Hills wearing my new footwear.

How would my mistress find me, her lady's maid, now—this new Hope that I am? What would she think of me? Full of Hope. And nothing of Clementine wearing these shoes of soft deerskin.

My mind makes me wonder whose hands crafted this leather from the skin of a deer for a foot such as mine.

Later, when we camp, the woman whose child Momma inquired about so long ago and so far back comes to our campsite this night carrying the child with her.

"I am Anna. Can you help him?" she asks, motioning the child toward Momma. Momma reaches for the limp bundle the woman holds.

Momma coos and hums to the young one as she takes the bundle in her arms.

"He is burning up with fever," Momma says. "How long?" But the woman is only silent. She shakes her head looking at the ground.

For a while, Momma doctors on the baby as best as she can. To give the woman hope, she holds the child up so it can see its mother's face. The child offers a weak smile as it looks at her. But all the while I wonder, and I know Momma does as well, why the woman waited so long to ask for help that had already been offered.

"I have never met a Negro," the woman says again, and stands, staring, over what is left of her child. Momma wraps the child in a clean cloth and hands the still and silent bundle back to his mother.

"What is his name?" Momma asks.

"Lucas," the woman answers.

Then, the father—we discover his name is Thomas—appears at our camp with their other three children. He bids us to follow him to a spot where a hole has been dug at the bottom of a juniper tree. The hole is being covered with dirt, and we place boulders over the spot as his father sings a song. The mother weeps and allows Momma to help hold her up. I tend the other children. Then the father takes a knife out of his pocket and carves the child's name into the tree. The parents and their children come back to our campfire with us.

They sit with Momma and talk about their child, Lucas. I play a game with their other children.

I pick up a small rock from the ground nearby. I show it to the children. Then I put it behind my back. I hide the rock in one of my hands. As I move my closed hands from behind my back, I ask, "Where is the rock?" They are supposed to guess the hand where the rock is hidden. As we play this game, I think about my own young self, back at Belle Hills Farm.

Listening to the children's squeals of laughter, I make a silent wish. Somehow, I wish whether people have seen the likes of my kind or not, I am allowed to be who I am—first a human being, who, like them, who is only *being human*. And I can keep these happy feelings I have at this moment. And my mind says to me: *Yes*, Hope. *The meaning of your name rests inside you. Look around you.*

I look around to hear the laughter of Momma and Poppa and Mister Jason as well. They are sitting and talking together with the man and woman. All are drinking the coffee and eating the sweet bread Momma offers them and their children. *Yes*, I say to my wandering mind. *This is something I can add into myself for Momma's hope and my own.*

Tonight, the people in the wagon party sing the "Home Sweet Home" song again. Along with the children, we all sing before it is time to end this day.

Over this next distance of many, many miles, we pass
creeks and rivers, steep hills that we must climb or
descend, and highlands and lowlands until we come
to Greasewood Creek and the Sweetwater River. One
mile or so farther, we come to an important destination point.

We arrive at Independence Rock on July third.
This is a most curious thing that I have seen on this
route. It covers about one hundred acres and is 250
feet high. There are more names—thousands of
names of emigrants that are painted or etched into
the rock. Some names are dated 1836. We all stop
and do the same.

I do not feel afraid to be seen writing, even though
what I am doing may be unlawful in some places like
Virginia and St. Louis. There is no log cabin jail here.
Like the others, I take a stone lying at the bottom of
the rock. Momma smiles and watches me write our
names along with the year 1849.

"That is good," she says. "Now all will know I have
been somewhere!"

After traveling so long for so many days to reach
this place, we are happy to camp and rest.

The next day, July fourth, we will not take the trail.
Instead, Mister Walter announces he has brought
a copy of the Declaration of Independence for this

moment. We are all told to gather and make part of a circle around the rock. Then he begins reading out loud. Speaking so close up to and against the rock makes his voice very big. His words boom off the stone walls. It is a moment for me to remember for all of my life.

"'When in the course of human events,'" he begins. I love hearing these words. They have a pretty and gentle sound to them. *The course of human events.* I will think about these words more when there is nothing ahead of me but the dreariness of the road.

Then he comes to the part in the reading that stirs something inside me. I reach out each of my hands to Momma and Poppa. I know the same thing stirs inside them. We squeeze one another's hands as Mister Walter continues:

> *"'We hold these truths to be self-evident*
> *that all men are created equal,*
> *that they are endowed by their Creator*
> *with certain unalienable Rights,*
> *that among these Rights are Life,*
> *Liberty,*
> *and the pursuit of Happiness.'"*

Momma and Poppa and I have never heard these words before . . . words that created this nation. The

United States of America. They are beautiful. Each word puts a picture in my mind. I remember my friend Miss Phillis Wheatley and her letter-poem to General George Washington, who led the fight for this country's freedom. I tell myself again it is a complex patchwork design that makes this curious quilt.

I look up and see our new family friends, Anna and Thomas and their children. We wave to each other and smile. Then we see Mister Jonathan Lincoln George, who is all smiles and who waves to us too.

Then the whole company, including Momma, Poppa, and I, all sing together "My Country, 'Tis of Thee." It is an easy song to learn.

"My country, 'tis of thee
Sweet land of liberty
Of thee I sing,
Land where my fathers died
Land of the pilgrims' pride,
From every mountainside,
Let freedom ring."

I look at Poppa, who wipes his eyes. And Momma. My eyes are full, and I can hardly see her face, but I know there are tears in her eyes too. Then we walk closer to the side of the rock, and she tells me with a sniffle, "Hope, in this spot, please write your mistress's name here." She points and holds her finger to the place where she wants it. "I have carried her with me through this adventure journey," Momma says. "Spell the letters out loud to me as you write them, my daughter. I want to know what they look like."

"E. L. I. Z. A. B. E. T. H," I say as I spell and write.

"Leave the word 'Elizabeth' behind," Momma says. "Yes. We will leave the word there where it is written and carry it no farther."

Leave the word "Elizabeth" behind? *Yes*, I think. Mister Cooper was right to remind us how this road changes a person. I wonder in which ways Momma and Poppa are changing.

It has been a good day. A new feeling of liberty and independence and openness blows in the warming winds and swirls around me, around us all. We are in the wilderness far away from the homes we all know, but in this place, even if it is just a moment, it feels like a home. And there is no place else like it.

Where we stop this night, near our encampment, we are still very close to the river crossing where stands Independence Rock. From a distance, it is a very grand thing to look back at. It stands on the plain, all by itself. Farther to the left, as well as on the right, there are mountains. But it stands on its own. I think of the thousands of names written on its walls. In my mind I smile. I am happy the names are there so that this rock that means so much to so many does not stand alone. Today, something big and wide as this wilderness stirs inside my heart.

"Elephant," I whisper. And I let the wind carry the word with it. Now my heart is light.

We keep moving. We come to a place where there is a huge crack in the wall of mountain. It is called Devil's Gate. It brings with it a great noise, as below it flows the Sweetwater River. Though I am tired, the sights of what we have seen and done take my breath away. This road is good where we travel. Then we enter a very narrow canyon. There are walls of rock on either side of us. In this valley the walls of rock go straight up and are as high as four hundred feet. "Or more . . . maybe," Poppa says.

Along the way there are broken-down wagons and what is left of dead oxen and horses. Within this place we cross the river twice.

As the road turns from the river bottom, toward a higher plane, we come into contact with wild sage. And crickets. So many crickets. The sound is deafening. I do not know which is worse, their chirping sound upon the ear, to have them jump from the ground to perch upon you, the crunching sound of their bodies under feet, hooves, and wagon wheels, the sight of them blanketing the ground, or the smell of them. It does not sit easy on the stomach.

On the banks of the Sweetwater River is a small stream of clear water. This country is barren, and the grass is short. There is no wood. There is only wild sage and, thankfully, buffalo chips. This adds to the weariness of the travelers. But we are surrounded by more rock shapes that are something to gaze upon. The imagination does not have to wander too far. There are shapes that resemble castles with turrets and a dome. But then, as you come closer, the pictures have disappeared into broken and formless masses of rock.

In some places the water has dried up, leaving deposits of bicarbonate of soda. "That is saleratus," Momma says, and begins to collect some of it.

"It is good for stomachaches and cooking," she says. But we cannot allow the team animals to drink this water.

We are now at a place on the plain near a river, more than ten miles from water. Here the sage grows as high as the top of your head. My weariness is taken away by the sighting of prairie dogs. They are funny to watch in their play of hide-and-seek with each other.

I have never seen such a creature as this. A prairie dog is about the size of a squirrel. Unlike squirrels, they make their homes in burrows under the sagebrush, not among the trees. They disappear inside their homes at the least sight of danger. There are so many that some of the boys and men knock them over with sticks or use pistols to capture dinner.

"They are fat and very oily," Momma says. "But I think I'd rather refer to the little critter as a prairie *squirrel* before I go to the trouble of cooking it and feeding it to you."

Tonight, for supper, after Poppa cleans them, Momma prepares them for eating. First, she sets them in water to boil, to get rid of some of the fat. Then she roasts them over the fire with salt, pepper, and some of the wild herbs she collected nearby. It needs a good amount of salt and pepper for flavoring it.

Mister Walter is not one to worry about things that happen on the trail, such as running out of this important seasoning. He has instructed us what to do should you run out of salt and pepper. "When you run out, get a light burn on the meat by placing it right into the fire. Take it off the fire. Then to season the meat, use a sprinkling of gunpowder. I guarantee it will taste the same." I am happy we have not run out of salt as some others in our wagon.

The evening mealtime is resting time as well. It is the part of the day I enjoy best. We sometimes talk of the wonders of the trail or what may occur tomorrow. It is an easy time, filled with good talk.

"Thank you, Addy," Mister Jason begins. "My father, God rest his soul, loved your cooking. You have turned these little wild prairie d . . . uh, squirrels into a very good meal. It is most enjoyable. I do like it a lot."

"It sure did make for such a tasty dinner," Poppa agrees.

As we cross the south bank of the Sweetwater, the land westward is a desert of sage and unfit water for the animals. In the middle of this barren land Poppa gets a certain look on his face.

"It seems to me that water should be near," he says. He takes the spade, a small shovel, from the side of the wagon. He walks away from our train. Then he sets to digging in the grasses.

After a short while, Mister Jason joins him, along with four other men and boys.

Then Poppa calls out. "Ice! Instead of water, we have ice!"

Everyone comes running, overjoyed to fill their buckets with the frozen water. This wilderness is such a strange world of things. Here in this hot, dry, sandy, and barren flat land, we find ice!

"I see you found the secret that ice is here," Mister Walter says to Poppa and Mister Jason. And there is laughter.

CHAPTER EIGHT

The Long, Hard Road

At the South Pass, where we camp, near Pacific Springs, Mister Cooper tells us news many have been waiting to hear.

"We have now crossed over to the Pacific side of this country," he says. "That means we are more than half the way to California! Congratulations! It won't be too much longer now!"

I begin a smile. Someone yells, "Amen!" Now laughter is heard. Whoops are shouted. Some of the emigrants dance around.

"Hurray!" someone yells. Then the company shouts all together, "Hurray! Hurray!" There is much joy and goodwill and laughter.

Someone brings our country's flag from their wagon to stake into the ground. Mister Cooper laughs and also raises his hand in a cheer. A man brings out his fiddle, another gets his trumpet. They play the song "My Country, 'Tis of Thee." Some people salute the flag. Others dance and sing and march around the flag. Then the fiddler starts to play "Carry Me Back to Ole Virginny." We all stop and yell out complaints. The fiddler laughs and then begins to play "Oh! Susannah!" and we are singing and dancing and cheering again.

When things settle down this night, Mister Cooper brings us together. He calls this meeting to prepare us for the next part of the journey.

"There is no one single *best* way west from here," he begins. "So that you know what is up ahead, I am aiming to take the path to what is called Sublette Cutoff and then to Hudspeth Cutoff. We will continue to make our way southwest from there. We travel the Humboldt Trail, along the Humboldt River. It's rough and hilly territory, but we will come to a spot that shouldn't be missed.

"Some call it 'Beer Springs,'" he says. There is laughter. "Don't get too excited." He chuckles. "Most know it as Soda Springs. It will be here we will take the Hudspeth Cutoff and on to Steeple Rocks. This may be a more rugged way, but it sure saves time.

"Now, some wagon companies will head south and around Salt Lake City, and that is fine and good. But there is much competition for water and grass there. And sometimes people can see how good the living can be there, they won't travel farther than that. I made a commitment to you, to this company. We are going all the way west to California!" More cheering rings out. Mister Cooper laughs, waiting for the company to quiet.

"I have taken many routes west and I have found

there is just no one best way. And like I stated, the way that I am choosing is a hard, rough road—we'll eventually find flat land again, and when we reach Bear River Valley in about two weeks' time, you will see it was worth it.

"There will be clear water and grassy meadows, hunting and fishing, geese and ducks, and trout. I tell you this so you will know what to expect along the way. Now get some sleep. You will need your rest!"

As I settle to sleep this night, my thoughts do not stop. I feel ready to go on.

At around eight o'clock, we began preparations. There is still a very good feeling in our camp. Voices are excited and loud. There is laughter, and spirits are high, yet the people move slowly. Then the call finally comes. "Move out! Move out on the trail!" We start the long march.

The road rises slowly and gradually. It is a strange thing to realize that soon we are in the Wind River Mountains. The peaks are covered with snow.

Then we start the descent along the Pacific Springs, which is also steep. There is not much feed here for the animals. The ground is sandy and covered with sage brush and waters that are alkaline. Some parts along this road are strewn with the bodies of oxen and the sickly sweet smell that lingers and you cannot forget. We travel this way for many miles.

Farther west we reach Dry Sandy River. Here we can water our animals and fill our canteens and water barrels. Some miles from this place we stop to sup and feed the teams. At sundown we start our night travel. We pause only to eat and then continue the march throughout the night.

We take Sublette Cutoff. There are more note sticks in the ground from others who have come this way. Some tell their friends who are behind them on the trail to "hurry up." I am grateful for these notes. It takes the loneliness out of this mountain way. Where we camp, we are once again able to fill our water supplies. There is not much for the team animals to eat. We are taught to make a mixture of hay, meal with flour, and water. The animals seem to enjoy the mash.

We arrive at Little Sandy at daylight. There is water and little food for the animals. We set up camp here and rest. We start again soon enough.

We travel this way two days. We reach Green River Valley—a beautiful valley with much grass—good for feeding the animals and there is fresh water.

As we travel the wide stretch of plains, a fine view presents itself. There are no particular landmarks except the Wind River Mountains. Snow covers the

tops of the mountains like little white hats. The peaks stand out under a ceiling of clouds. On one side of us the road changes its direction, and we can see the cliffs of the Sweetwater fading in the distance. We see more people along the way. These are known as Pottawattamie. They are dressed in beautiful clothes of buckskin and beads. Poppa stares at their handsome ponies as the Pottawattamie lead them past us on the road.

The open country lies before us. There are dangers of quicksand. The face of the wilderness is peculiar, like nothing I could ever imagine. Red earth columns suddenly rise up from flat ground. Antelope, buffalo, lizards, crickets, insects crawling over the burning sand. As weary as my eyes may be, I cannot get enough of what I am seeing. I wonder what Mistress would think of all of these wild and wide-open spaces.

The rivers rise in the Wind River Mountains. The melting snows gives the water an icy coldness. It is sweet and good to taste. The only fire fuel is cottonwood trees and willow bushes. But they grow sparsely. Everything is sand. Momma says there is no good ground for growing things.

We come to a river we must cross. The waters are swift and swollen. It does not seem to have any banks.

The wagon beds are raised so they won't dip into the water.

"Sit at the back of the wagon," Poppa tells Momma and me. "The weight will help to steady it." My mind is moving as fast as the river. "Do not be afraid," Poppa says.

I hold tight to the side of the wagon. On this journey I have not known so much fear, or the fear I became used to living in the household with Mister Uncle. Daily I felt threatened I would be sold away from those I love. Somehow, I do not hold *that* fear in *this* world, being so close to Momma and Poppa. Mister Jason would not threaten to sell us while we are on the road depending on each other for survival. The loud voices of the men rise up over the water as they call and lash their whips to drive the poor animals. Riding through the surging water and over the quick sands is something I know I will never forget.

We continue to roll through the sunbaked days through the foothills of the Bear River Mountains. We wind through dusty ridges and descend through sand and grit. The nights are very cold. Ice forms in our water buckets. The days are very hot.

When we reach the creek bottom, there is good grass for the animals. It is nice that we have a level road here.

Bear River Valley has many rugged hills. Yet we are

able to find grass for the grazing animals in hollows along the way. There are mountain sheep on these hills. It is such a sight to see how they climb and to hear the clacking of their hooves on the stone.

From these bluffs we see the Green River in front of us. It is a welcome sight. Before we can get to the stream our team becomes impatient. As it is safe to do so, Poppa wheel-locked the wagon so we move slowly down the hill. Then Poppa lets the team loose from their yokes and tethers to stop them from stampeding down and rushing into the water. The sight is beautiful. I am happy the poor animals can take long drinks and cool their tired feet. Like them, I do the same.

I take off my moccasins. The cold feels good on my feet. I know I will remember this. Here the water is very clear and we see the fish. Many of us find this funny. There are yelps and peals of laughter.

"Get out your fishing poles," someone yells.

"But I didn't bring one," voices yell back.

"Then use your hands!" someone else adds, and laughter is heard for the first in a most long time.

All in the company set out to catch fish. Some use fishing poles they have brought along. Others turn sticks into spears, or tie sticks together with twine, or use their bare hands. The mood is lively and quick, just like a stream of swimming fish. I know there will be good cooking smells, singing, and music tonight. And I am happy for this.

Where we camp there are trees of all kinds. As far as you can see are mountains—one after another. So many trees. And much beauty. I say to myself, *This makes it all so much worth it.*

What? my mind says to me.

Beauty, I say back to my mind. I think back hard on all of this road and all of this way we have come, and I say to myself, *As hard as everything along this long way is on the body, the mind is the thing that will not suffer when you can see such things as this. Beauty that is all around you cannot be . . .* And then I have no words in my mind to say anything more, so I sleep. I know I will remember these days of my life for all time.

And as I drift off, I hear Poppa laughing. "It is going to be a trick to get the teams back into their yokes. But it will be worth the trouble for them to be happy." Poppa chuckles.

Mister Walter says we will continue to travel at night as much as we can. On this path called Sublette Cutoff are more note sticks in the ground. We camp near here for the night. We are told that tomorrow or the next day we will come to Bear River. It is said to be a curiosity. We ascend another range near a good road to walk. We travel along the stream for some miles, and we camp in this valley. I do not sleep much. I set my sights on the promise of water at our next place.

As we set out that morning, there is not much here, but we continue on. The trail is a dry powder. Walking hooves, turning wheels, and stepping feet kick up clouds of dust. It is a miserable feeling to get it in your eyes and nose. Still, I am in good spirits.

This day the sun beats down all around us. There is some wind, but it blows hot as well and offers no relief. We move through a powdery fog.

In the distance, from these hilly lands, we can see the Green River. It is a beautiful and welcome sight. The animals sense the water is near. They show their eagerness to find it. The closer we get, their excitement gets greater and greater. They hurry us down the mountain slope to the river. Finally, Poppa sets our team loose from their yokes and tethers.

It is good to see the animals cooling their feet in the water and drinking as much as they want. I am happy to camp here for two nights to rest and restore.

As my eyes close for the night, I know I will be sad to leave this place in two days' time.

Today we start early. We climb other mountains and steep hills. The country is beautiful. There are grass and flowers. The river provides much trout to eat.

I am happy to camp here.

This new day, we break camp early. We leave the river, and the road we are on now is known as Hudspeth Cutoff, Mister Walter says. In a day's time we should make our way to Steeple Rocks. I know why he tells us these things ahead of time—so our spirits remain high.

Early this morning we start the road again. Our travel is over high and narrow ridges. The progress is slow. There are more note sticks to tell us what is ahead. Dust rises in clouds, covering everything. We make little progress.

This day, we begin the trail around nine o'clock. We do not have to travel far before we come to the special place Mister Cooper told us about. It proves to be true—a most curious place. At nooning we stop at Soda and Beer Springs. There we see two pointed mounds. Poppa says they are about twenty feet high. These springs are water that come up from under the ground. They bubble and fizz and hiss as they burble up from the earth. The water tastes like soda water. It simmers and foams like it is boiling. Momma says it is perfect for baking bread. The springs are rather more than half a mile north of the road, and near them is a fine brook, lined with cedars, which runs into the river a mile or two below.

Our guides say these springs are great luxuries. They are delicious and refreshing to drink.

"If only I had lemon," Mister Walter teases. "I'd refuse the sugar if I could have the lemon. It would be the best-tasting lemon soda in the world." He laughs.

Some miles below here are at least a dozen more of these springs. Near the edge of the river are some that are even stronger. I must admit, it is funny to hear the water making such odd noises. One spring looks to be a boiling pot of water. These springs roil and hiss and foam. We find a creek among these hills at the Bear River. There is good feed here. We stop and camp here for dinner. Then we move on some miles away to camp for the night.

Again today, we start the trail early. Mister Walter says we make good progress. As we leave our nooning stop, we come to a couple of fellows on horseback. They bring news of a horrible tragedy.

In the middle of May, there was a dreadful fire in the great city of St. Louis. The firestorm started on the steamboat the *White Cloud*. This is the very boat whose name I so admired that sat alongside the *Robert Campbell*, which brought our company to Missouri.

To make the matter worse, hard, dry winds came in, which blew the flames and embers, causing it to spread along the crowded boat landing and into the streets beyond. Twenty-three steamboats were destroyed and most of the freight and parcels that lay upon the landing incinerated. Four hundred eighteen buildings burned. The fire lasted two long days.

In the end, three people perished in the flames. It just added to the misery of the number of persons who died from cholera. In all, with the city blaze and disease combined, 4,317 souls were lost. This is such sad, sad news. I am only grateful we were not there to witness it or to have been one of the unlucky ones.

I take a moment to think on this. I find myself looking behind me again and again—looking back from where we have come. I wonder on this. *Why?* I ask my mind. And now I have been given the answer. This life we live is like the patchwork in the quilt coverings we use at Belle Hills. Just like the quilt, which is a mixture of fabric patterns, life is like a jumble of things. There is good and bad and easy and hard. The ground you stand upon, gazing at the patchwork, gives you a chance to make sense of it and judge your own mind while you are wrapped up in the quilt of your past and the life you have lived. I keep looking back to see now where I stand.

These opposite things are so hard to hold inside the mind to understand. I clutch my volume of Miss Wheatley's poems as I walk, letting my thoughts wander as I think of these things, and I realize something inside me needs to change.

We continue the trail. Here the wagon ruts are thinner. This path is not very well known or used. But there are many more note sticks and cards that promise this will take us to the Humboldt River in only one hundred miles. Mister Walter says much of this territory is new and still unnamed. Mister Cooper is heartened that he will meet a friend along this way. This encouragement of something familiar is helpful for us all.

It is good that not every moment is burdened with death and pain, which leaves the body and heart weary and drained. There are some happy times and thoughts. It is curious that some emigrants have seen fit to give their wagons a name. We see such names as "Star Along," "Living Hoosier," "Ready and Rough," "The Dowd Family," "Buffaloes," and "Gold Hunters" painted on the cloth bonnets of the wagons. This evening at supper Mister Jason asked if we should do the same and paint a name on our wagon.

"What should we call ourselves?" Mister Jason asks.

"Argonauts!" I chime in without thinking. "Just like in the story." We all chuckle. And so, since then, not only are we wagon number nine, but we are also known as argonauts.

And so, it is decided. Mister Jason has bartered with another wagon. We are exchanging tea for a brush and paint. Extra supplies of coffee and tea or any necessary food on this trail can be used for bartering and are as good as money.

"We have a choice of red or black paint," Mister Jason says.

Momma chooses black. "That paint color is a better choice here in this wilderness . . . though blue in this wild place would be nice too," she says.

We borrow a ladder, and it is Mister Jason who must paint the letters. He is happy to oblige to fulfill his idea.

There is enough black paint to place an underline under the word "ARGONAUTS," which makes it stand out even more.

"Nice work, argonauts," Mister Cooper and Mister Walter tell us as they are cantering beside our wagon as we walk. These words buzz inside me. I am not a servant or a lady's maid on this trail. Although I do everything I can to serve in my station, I am also something more. I am an argonaut, an adventurer seeking treasure of my own. Not gold. But what would be the greatest treasure for me? I know what this is.

I am glad for this name. It keeps our spirits high.

There are many here we see along the trail. They call themselves mountain men. They serve as guides, animal trappers, and fur traders. They are rugged in appearance and manner and are dressed in buckskin and fur of beaver. Farther up the trail, Mister Cooper will meet and talk with a mountain man who is a friend.

"This man knows this terrain like he knows his own face," Mister Walter tells us. Hearing this makes me feel happy that this journey for some is familiar. It takes away some of its wilderness.

The next day we leave camp early within sight of snow-topped mountains. Along the way we pass many teams who tell us there is plenty of grass, wood, and water all the way through. Everyone is happy to hear this news.

We meet a company of Mormon people. They are headed to the Great Salt Lake. Others in their group have already settled there. They tell us they are building a city for themselves that will be their home.

Today, Mister Cooper is happy that we traveled twenty-three miles.

At our supper this night, as we eat this meal, Mister Jason suddenly begins reaching into his pockets.

"Hope," Mister Jason says. "I have something I have been carrying . . . for you . . . If I can find it . . . in one of my many . . . pockets."

When he cannot easily find it, he places his dinner plate on the ground and stands with a smile as he goes from pocket to waistcoat pocket before he finally retrieves what he has been searching for.

"This is for you." He takes the item and holds it out to me.

"What is it?" I ask.

"It is a letter from Mother, your mistress," he says. "It was included within my bundle. I discovered it inside my Bible when I had cause to read it some days ago. True to my word, I have not opened it or read it, and do not know what she has said to you." He smiles.

"But . . ." And he changes his tone to a more fevered pitch. "If she is contracting you to spy upon my doings, as she had you do when we were children, I will not have it!" Then he softens his tone to me again and smiles.

I swallow hard, taking the letter.

"Do I have to read it now? Aloud?"

"Read it when and where you please. It is your letter. . . ."

A *letter*? I think. I have never received a letter before. I do not know who besides Mistress would ever write a letter to me. My mind is so full of this word, "letter," I can hardly hear what he is saying.

". . . only remember my warning to you," he says as he raises a finger of caution.

Momentarily I hold Mistress's letter in my hand. I look at the handwriting and the form of the alphabet letters. It resembles and is so much like my own, as it was she who taught me to write. I have not put pen to paper since before our journey began.

I turn to Poppa and Momma. "Would you like for me to read it to *you*?"

They both nod to agree with Mister Jason. "It is your letter. It was written to you," Momma says. Poppa smiles.

I reach into my pocket for my volume. I place the letter on the opening page of my book.

"I have never received a letter from my mistress before—or *anyone* before." I giggle. And I realize how far away from my home we have come. But I do not feel lonesome for Belle Hills.

"I will read it later," I say softly before returning to my meal.

This night, as I lie down to sleep, my mind begins to wander back to the words Mister Walter read:

We hold these truths to be self-evident
that all men are created equal . . .

My mind thinks of these words. I read in the newspapers while at Belle Hills of this "most peculiar and curious life" we who are bondspeople live and the ties we have with them. These writings have made me think about the relations we hold to our mistress and have with the Barnett family—the way we feel about each other and how we behave toward each other.

Even here, all along the trail, and in the state of Virginia, we live together, and so close together with each other—as close and near as the heart and blood knits those within a family. We occupy the same rooms and yet the outside color of our skin keeps us so distant and far apart. It is a confusing thing to understand. "Peculiar," the article said.

Just as I am closing my eyes, I see a picture of Mistress's letter to me. "To Clementine" is written on the envelope holding the letter.

Around us the land is barren, but our hopes are to find good feed soon enough. We drive on and we come to a low area of land. The feed here is little and poor. This valley, Mister Walter says, goes on for some miles. We travel this way for most of the day and into the night. When we finally camp, it is on a dry creek bank. There is dry grass but no water.

On this day, as we travel, antelope and mountain sheep roam beside the trail. They are not wild. It makes for easy hunting and is a welcome change from bacon. They are delicious to eat.

There are times of excitement but mostly it is routine and dreariness. It can be hard for some to bear. At times it has been difficult for me. Some have become weary of the road that seems it will never end. Mister Walter tells us it is at these times that people have wandered off from the wagon in the night and are never seen again. After hearing this, I do my best to keep my spirits high. Sometimes, with one hand holding to the wagon, I am able to carry my little volume with the other hand. I read from it as we walk along the flat, dry land.

In this way, I have committed one of Miss Wheatley's poems to memory. It is called, "On Being Brought from Africa to America." I marvel how time passes around us. It was published in 1773, seventy-six years ago.

I admit it has made a part of this dullness bearable.

This is Miss Wheatley's poem:

On Being Brought from Africa to America

'Twas mercy brought me from my *Pagan* land,
Taught my benighted soul to understand
That there's a God, that there's a *Saviour* too:
Once I redemption neither sought nor knew.
Some view our sable race with scornful eye,
"Their colour a diabolic dye."
Remember, *Christians*, *Negros*, black as *Cain*,
May be refin'd, and join th' angelic train.

I have read this poem so many times, I am able to say it without looking at the words in my little book. Miss Wheatley's poem is so dear to me. It rests upon my heart for so many hundreds and hundreds of miles. While I remember it, my wandering mind causes me to think hard about her words and what they mean. And it has caused me to think of myself and put myself inside her poem.

Sometimes when I am reciting her verse along the trail, my mind has done a most curious thing. It is causing me *to change* her words to suit me as I travel here so long on this tedious journey. And though it relieves my heart mightily, this is also a great worry for me.

Mistress was right long ago when she said my mind

is able to grab hold of words and wrestle them for my understanding. I have done this with Miss Wheatley's words. Now I pray my dear Miss Wheatley, who I am sure is resting in heaven, will not hold hard against me my wrongdoing to her dear, beloved poem. I hope she will forgive me. I hope she will see that what I am doing with her poem is only helping to save my own life. For it has kept me from wandering off—away from Momma and Poppa and our camp in the middle of the night as some unfortunate others have done.

CHAPTER NINE

Sierra Nevada Mountains— The Donner Party

August 21, 1849, to September 24, 1849
The Humboldt River through the Desert of the Great Basin

Being so close to the Pacific Ocean, the roads, the weather, and the land have changed mightily. There is heat and no rain. The colors of the earth have changed from muddy, or black soil, to baked brown sand. When the air blows, it gives no relief. Mister Walter has taken to tracking the weather on a thermometer. I declare there are times I wish he would find another pastime. Today the heat reached 104 degrees. Though Momma says she is glad to know the temperature.

"I have never been in a desert," she says. "I have never known heat such as this, and I do not know when I will again."

Uneasiness grows in our group as the hot air, grit, and dust rise with every step. But it is worse on the animals that carry us. The walk on the soft sand is more difficult than walking on the hard, uneven ground. But by now I am weary of this walk too. We have gone over sandy places before, but this seems to be forever. Each time I place my foot down, the ground gives way underneath me. My feet and legs have to work harder to keep me from falling. I hold to the side of the wagon sometimes to keep me steady.

There are more things that cause worry and flare tempers. Mister Cooper calls for another company meeting. There is something new we must be ready for. At our camp this night Mister Cooper tells us about this next difficult passage.

"Where we are now, these trails, we must take great precautions when allowing team animals to drink. Much of these pools—this water—is alkaline," Mister Cooper tells us. "We will have to guard the cattle so that they do not wander off and drink the bad water. There is nothing worse than the sight of watching these poor animals suffer a horrible end."

"These roads are more rugged than any we have seen yet. The water will not be so good. I tell you this to help you to prepare for what is ahead. You may consider unloading other unnecessary items. Lessen the weight to make it easier on your team animals and replace it with good clean water when we find it. But take heart. Don't lose yourselves.

"This next part of the way will be a big push to get to the California gold diggings. It will be another kind of challenge. We will continue to move due west into rougher country. And it can be done. Many before you have done this. There is no reason why you can't. Our greatest push of all will be yet to come—to cross the Great Basin where we will be surrounded by a sea of deserts. We follow the

Humboldt River along the Humboldt Trail. Some call it the 'Humbug River.'"

"A friend of mine says it is also called the Forty Mile Desert," the man who plays the fiddle says. Some of the emigrants laugh.

"I'm glad to see you have a good disposition about this," Mister Cooper says, and chuckles, too. "Yes, you will see for yourself. We'll pick up the Carson Trail at the end of the Humboldt Sink. When the Humboldt River dries out, what is left is the sunken dry bed called a sink, where the land drops down. Things will be a little better for us for a while getting to the Carson River through Carson Valley. It's rugged and rocky, but it is a pretty canyon. About seven miles or so, we reach what is called Hope Valley. And it is as good as the name sounds."

Hope Valley, I think. I feel most of my worry leave me. *Hope*, I say to myself. *Yes.*

"Whatever you end up calling it, it is a rough trail," Mister Cooper continues. "I tell you this so you know what you will be up against. Prepare yourselves.

"Sometimes because of the heat, we will turn things around. We will be traveling at night through the deserts. We'll sleep as best as we can during the day.

"I know many of you, for other reasons, worry about this stretch of the trail. You will do wise to let those thoughts go and think only of what is in front of you—the gold diggings of California and the fertile fields of the Sacramento Valley. Some call it an Eden that is worth waiting for.

"Finally, I say to you: Knowing what it has been like to travel through a hell on earth, will it be worth it to you to know heaven for the rest of your lives? Mock my words, but our destination is a valley of plenty."

"A valley of plenty," Momma mumbles. I like the sound of that too. But what will that mean for my family? For me? I wonder.

"I would like very well to see how that looks," Momma says.

Still, people in our company cannot help but to say out loud their worries of traveling the same path as the unfortunate party who were lost in the Sierra Nevada Mountains. Mister Jason is confident Mister Cooper understands this and knows the roads. Poppa too is confident of this man's knowledge. He has consulted all maps available that cover the route.

Other worries spring up about this river. It is feared as much as the mountains of the Sierra. Mister Walter says our concerns are misplaced. The desert is a most difficult passage. We will get through those mountains well before any winter storms. Somehow, I feel joy to hear this.

Mister Cooper tells Mister Jason and some of the men it is on this part of the trail where we will finally meet up with his good friend the mountain man. He is a guide who knows these trails best. Mister Cooper is very happy about this.

During this day's journey, the country is very dry. Everywhere, we come to water that is very salty. In one place the water has a foul smell and is not fit to use. The sun blazes. Eventually, after many miles, we arrive at a pond and again the water is unfit to drink.

Coming to a temporary trading post we see a sign near the road labeled POST OFFICE. This man-made post office is not what it seems. A notice is attached letting travelers know they will "carry letters & c." for a price, "half a dollar." Mister Cooper warns us that many a half-dollar might be left with the parcel, but their friends on the other end would never read or receive such a note.

Although the days are warm, the night brings frost. In the morning the sun sparkles, giving a shimmering look to the ice-covered ground.

We have arrived at Steeple Rocks. All around us this morning are sights of hills and mountains covered with snow. It is a dangerous and steep mountain pass. It is frightful. On these descents, it is very slow going. The hind wheels must be chained and each wagon steadied with long ropes. Thankfully, each helps another. I think it is a good thing most of our supplies are used up and these wagon loads are not as heavy as when we started. We have nooning time here, but there is no feed for the teams. I am happy we camp early.

My mood remains happy this morning when we break camp. The road runs over a rolling, bleak section of ground. When we camp tonight, our company is in good spirits, having come so far. There is some grass. Some talk in anxious whispers for the time when the Sierra Mountains will come into view. I declare, I cannot let myself think too much of how we have come so close to the place of great heartbreak and tragedy that I read about to Mistress in our home in Virginia. And now, I, my mistress's lady's maid, am near to that very place. I declare, I think, elephants show themselves everywhere and in so many ways on this journey.

We come to a muddy river for nooning time. There is little feed for the teams. The animals do poorly. I am glad this road here in this place is flat and even.

This day, so many miles from Steeple Rocks, we arrive at a spring of warm water. We are coming to the place that is called Thousand Springs Valley.

Mister Walter says this is a fitting name for such a place. There are miles and miles of springs, water that comes up out of the ground. This land we pass through is marshy with pond water, most is unfit to drink. The first we come to is Warm Springs Valley. We leave the Warm Springs Valley as the sun finishes its time in the sky. We continue traveling until late at night. We camp on banks of a dry creek bed without grass or water for the animals.

We start early this morning, though I do not feel rested. My heart lightens when we finally find water for the animals. We come to another place of note, Hot Springs Valley. There is food for the animals, and water. We noon here and on the road, we come to Hot Springs. The road smooths out here, and where we camp, we find grass. This place, Hot Springs Creek, is a running stream.

On our route today, we come through a wondrous place. Here are springs that are clustered together, and they are boiling. The land is marshy. In the distance there is fog, as can happen sometimes in rainy weather back home in Virginia. My mind wonders if it is possible to have Virginia weather here in the desert, too. As we get closer, we see it is not fog from rain. It is cloudy puffs, gusts of steam that rise out of the ground. Hot Springs is a very good-sized place. There is good water and feed here.

In the early morning we continue to travel along the valley. We find more springs of boiling water. Momma laughs and says they are hot enough to cook an egg. Then we pass springs nearby of pure, cold water. I declare, this place holds so many mysteries. We travel all day and well into this night and we are happy, for our animals are well fed, and for now their thirst is quenched. Resting this night is easy.

Finally, just as our note stick friends promised, we reach the Humboldt River. It is also known as Mary's River, though I do not know why. It is here we take a long rest for our morning meal. There is time to forage, or hunt, for food. There is game: wild geese and sage hens. There are fish in the stream.

The Humboldt River is a crooked river. "It may be three hundred miles long," Mister Walter says.

"Maybe more." Mister Cooper chuckles.

Our guides say it will be a three-week journey. "Three weeks," Mister Cooper repeats. I know Poppa is thinking what I am thinking. *What happens then?*

Getting through the Great Basin will be the biggest push of all. We will get through the dreaded Forty Mile Desert.

There is little else but rugged, barren mountains. There is no grass to be seen. The water from the spring disappeared. Today, we travel during the night. This means we have breakfast late. There is nothing but broken country ahead of us. And we do as we have done before. We must keep moving across the basin.

We come to the springs in the Humboldt River Valley across the Great Basin. Thankfully, before we start through what Mister Cooper describes as the Forty Mile Desert, there are water, grass, and wood that are needed for the emigrants and the teams here. As we continue to go down the Humboldt, the water is still not fit for animals to drink. Then there are almost no trees, only firewood, broken brush, and dried grass.

The road is the same as the day before except it is more broken. A few miles from where we camped is some low meadowland. Near the river a sign reads, THE WATER HERE IS POISON!

"Do not let your cattle drink on this bottom," Mister Walter cries out. On our wagon train, we have already lost so many animals. One of our cattle does drink from the river. It will be a certain death.

Poppa calls to Momma and me, "Addy, Hope, we must act quickly. Bring bacon! Bring vinegar. Either one will do."

Momma and I bring both. I do not know what Poppa plans to do with our provisions at a time when the animal already shows signs of death. Saliva foam begins to flow freely from its mouth. Soon the animal's stomach will start to swell. It will grow weak and tremble. I do not know what Poppa can do to save the life of the beast now.

Momma and I hurry. Poppa grabs the vinegar from my hand. Momma holds the bacon slab. The animal is weak. I feel so sad for it. It does not know what is happening to it or what to do. The animal has no control of itself. It tries to walk and then sit down at the same time. Finally, it falls to its knees. Poppa grabs it around its neck to steady it.

"Help me, Hope. Help me to get the mouth to open."

Poppa and I work together to do this. Poppa takes the vinegar and pours it down the animal's throat and into its stomach. He then takes the bacon and does the same.

"Now we wait to see if we are not too late," Poppa says. He sends us back to our wagon. He stays with the animal to see if the remedy helped. The vinegar and pork should keep the dangerous water from killing the animal.

The next morning the animal is weak and will survive, but Poppa is not sure it is well enough when we move out. We have to leave this poor beast behind. This loss worries me greatly.

"I think we have enough food until we can resupply," Momma says, and I think what must be given up to make this journey.

Wherever we can find it, we take a supply of water for the walk across the desert. Every animal and person is more parched and thirsty than hungry. And we are just as tired, but stopping would mean death. We must keep going to find water. We are too close to the end to stop now.

We see along the way rotting carcasses of animals that were too tired to go farther. The horses lie down. The men cannot get them to move until they are given water. It feels like what death could be. My mind begins to wander. *Stop!* I say. I tell my wandering mind we will *not* die, not in this way. I will not wander away. And I only let myself think of Miss Wheatley, her freedom, and my poem.

From the road we travel on now, the Humboldt River is clearly in view. This is a most vital stream we will follow to take us to California. I see what Mister Cooper talked about. It is a dry and worrisome trek. Crossing along this trail doesn't seem like climbing a hill. The heat of the desert is hard on us all—animals and people. We will travel along this trail at night and sleep in the day when we can. It is cooler at night without the blazing sun.

When we camp, we find a good creek with some willow trees. It is difficult to sleep. At six o'clock, we start again. The night is cool. We travel twenty miles.

We find hens nesting in the brush. Mister Walter says they are sage hens. They fly in many directions. Momma thinks a pot pie would be tasty. The birds are about the same size as the chickens we have back home. I like the taste. It has been some days since we had fresh meat. But the food the animals can eat is not good.

This day we meet another group of Mormons heading to Salt Lake City. They have news of California. The captain of this camp talks to our captains and our wagon company. There is so much news, some welcome and some that brings more worry.

"There are hard roads ahead; there is little to no grass at the Humboldt Sink. Cut hay where you can to feed the teams while crossing the desert to Carson River. You will find good feed over the mountains, the prices of everything to buy are lower in California," they tell us. "You will find that the steamers are now running from San Francisco up the Sacramento River and to Sacramento City."

Hearing this news of California is good.

This day we left the camp late. The feeling of nervousness rises again along with the dust. Where we camp is five miles above the South Fork of the Humboldt River. All I can think this day is desert. More desert to come. We went twenty-two miles before we camped.

There are horse tracks and lodge pole trails on our path. Mister Walter says he cannot say for sure, but they might be from the Shoshone people. We set up for the night beside a muddy stream.

As we are traveling along this river, we see some people making their way alone without a company or wagons. We see a man on foot carrying a bow and arrow, which he tells us he uses to hunt antelope.

"They are a-plenty here, when you can get them," he says.

This day we make sixteen miles. We camp near alkaline water and very little grass. We use all our strength to keep the cattle away—it is very difficult.

* * *

All we can do is continue west. There is not much feed here and again the water is not fit for the animals to drink.

The roads are strewn with the bodies of dead oxen.

In spite of all the troubles on this journey, I tell myself to be happy with the hardness of walking this road. No day on this road is as hard as living in the house with Mister Uncle. I feel my volume moving in my pocket. And I remind myself of the letter I received from my mistress.

You must read it! I say to myself. Sooner or later, I must see what she has written to me, though I know I will read it through the eyes of this *new* Hope that I have become. Not Clementine. Never Clementine. *Only new Hope,* I say to myself. *Look how far you have come.* And then I discover that I am smiling to myself at the thought of my own name. *I am a new Hope,* I say to myself. And then I discover that I am laughing aloud at this thought of my name. *New Hope!*

CHAPTER TEN

Meeting Someone Familiar and New— Frontiersman Jim Beckwourth

When we stop, Momma makes tea to refresh us, but it has a sour and vinegary taste to it. But still, we hurry on. We go through miles of more of the same. And yet, this wilderness that is full of surprises such as ice in the desert surprises us even more. Each day everything that moves is in great need of water. Still, we must move on. Then we come across the most beautiful hills of colored earth that I could ever imagine. There are shades of pink, white, yellow, and green. The mountains around seem to all but glow. We continue west pressing on through the basin. After we climb another small hill, we hear Mister Cooper's shouting voice. He is at the front of the wagon train.

"I see where there is the spring! Just up ahead!"

I declare my feet do not seem as heavy as before. Somehow the tiredness leaves me, and I have excitement in my steps—for water.

We are now about ten miles beyond the desert mail station, Mister Walter tells us. Here a road turns off from the main trail toward a very high sandy ridge. We have come across the worst places of desert. There are still long roads of sand, and the land beyond is plain and barren. On the very north side is a large spring of fresh water. The animals are eager, but they move slowly. Some of the emigrants call this an oasis. It is beautiful. All the trains we saw along the trail encamp here. The animals are as worn out as the people.

On the East Fork of the Carson River, above the plains, toward the direction of our road, is a mountain full of vegetation, but there is a boiling water spring. We travel steadily as best we can. The emigrants in our company say we have found another oasis in the desert. A large source of water lies before us. It burbles up from the ground, and it is very hot. The water is very deep. Where it runs off is cool. The grasses around it are nearly all underwater. We take turns wading in it.

Momma says there is heated water that bubbles out of the ground near Belle Hills. Some say those waters heal the sick. "Back home, I have never seen them, but I have heard stories told about them. The waters have some things in it to heal rheumatism— that helps your aching bones."

Desert and mountains are all the eyes can see around us, but in this place we find better grass. There is also another spring filled with hot water. We are told of another some few miles ahead where it is a good place to camp. We head this way to give our cattle and team animals a place to rest.

Once we arrive, we look around and see a beautiful place of green grass that seems to go on forever. Momma says she could actually make coffee by setting the coffeepot into the boiling water.

During most of the day we drive on and on. We know we are so much closer to our stopping place. Mister Cooper shows the company the latest map of California and Oregon and where we are on the trail. Poppa and Momma take a great interest in seeing the map, but I do not. I am worried about what lies ahead for us, and whether Mister Jason would find his golden fleece. I do not know what it would mean for us.

I think Mister Cooper shows us the map to give hope. We know we have more dreary times up ahead. There is more of the worrisome desert to cross.

The sand is so deep for miles. By now we have less water. What we have has to be saved. We collected as much of the hot water from the boiling springs as we could. By nightfall and the time we camp, the water is cool enough to drink. It is such a sweet, cool drink. The next morning, we are up and traveling again through the deep sand.

During the daylight, all along the trail, you look

down at your feet to be sure of where you step. Or you look straight ahead of you to see where you are going or what surprises there are to see. But night is the time to look up. The sky glimmers with millions of pulsing stars. The heavens seem close enough to reach out your hand and touch. It is a wondrous sight. This too is its own kind of Garden of Eden. The desert, when it is empty of rotting animal carcasses, has a sweet smell.

"Sage," Momma says. "I will remember this one thing most about this journey. I love the smell of it."

Careful guard has to be kept during the night. Wild creatures can attack the team animals.

We come along to a great long stretch of mountains. I wonder what these mountains are called.

"The Sierra Nevada Mountains are in view," Mister Walter says. I stare at their beauty knowing what terrible thing occurred there. When we came upon a broad track, we see the peaks, the snow still lingers. The air feels cool, more like autumn than the heat of summer. We move toward the bottom of the great mountain over which we will pass. As we continue forward at the evening meal, Mister Jason reminds us we should soon be in the California mountains and close to the end of our tedious journey.

My mind and imagination wander and worry— a thousand worries flow through my head like a waterfall, but not one has presented itself during our travels. There are so many remarkable things about this trail. It is as if our company is seeing something new. In the ravines are plenty of wild cherries. They are not very good unless they are cooked. We collect some and Momma prepares them over an open fire.

At the foot of the mountain, we come upon a group of men. They are three in number. These men are not on the trail for the reasons we are. They are explorers, hunters, and fur trappers. Their voices have a deep heartiness and fearlessness about them that is new to me. At dinner tonight at our campsite, they join our group. These are the mountain men Mister Cooper talked of meeting somewhere along the trail. One of the men is his good friend.

I look at these men carefully. One of them, Mister Jim Beckwourth, stands out from the others. It is another case of "seeing the elephant." I have never seen such a man or known such a man as he could even exist.

He was born in the state of Virginia. If he still lived there, instead of exploring in the mountains, he would be an enslaved servant, just like Momma and Poppa and me. Though I do not believe those spaces back home could hold him. This man is fearless. He's big in size, which matches his boldness. It is hard to understand. I watch him carefully. Poppa regards him in the same way.

He is the first free person of my kind I have ever seen. I know of Mister Frederick Douglass. I know of Miss Phillis Wheatley—both are free. I see Mister Jim Beckwourth with my own eyes—and he seems a most different sort. Something inside me grows bigger than ever before. Then the thing that grows pours out from my eyes. I am so happy for the ones of us who have their liberty.

Everything about Jim Beckwourth is free. He is as wide and open as the wilderness. His voice booms and rattles to fill up the space around him. His laughter is deep and carefree. He comes to our camp to talk. He greets Poppa with a hearty handshake. He wants to talk with Poppa.

"I was born into slavery in Frederick County, Virginia," he begins. "I am the natural-born son of Sir Jennings Beckwourth and a bondswoman." He does not give his mother's name.

"My given name is James Pierson Beckwourth. When my father gave me my freedom, I learned the trade of blacksmith.

"My first exploring expedition west was the winter of 1824 to '25. I have never looked back."

"You never looked back? Don't you miss your

home in Virginia?" Poppa asks. I listen closely to what the man with the big voice says.

"Pshaw," he says. "Virginia is too small a place for me." I am happy to hear his words and to see how he and Poppa both laugh.

"I've come to feel at home in these big, wide-open spaces," he says, gesturing with his arms. "I see myself as a man of this frontier. You might see upon a return to Virginia that it has grown *too small* for you, too." He looks back and forth at Poppa and Momma. His words ring inside me.

"For now, California is free," he continues. "Though there is talk of adding it to the union, as yet it is not a slave-holding state. California is a big place." He looks at Poppa and laughs.

"California is a big place to hide," Mister Beckwourth says almost as a whisper. The words of his powerful voice and meaning hold in the air a few moments before he speaks again. My heart soars as high as the stars. While Poppa and he continue to talk, it is as if my thoughts have opened up and I know what I want my poem to say. I now call Miss Wheatley's poem "On Being Brought from Virginia to California":

On Being Brought from Virginia to California

'Twas mercy that brought me from Virginia
    land

Being on this road has taught my mind to
    understand
That through the ways of our God,
and the ways of our Savior too,
Can plant your feet to move upon the earth in
    places you never knew.
Some people here upon this wagon train
viewed my race with a scornful distrustful eye.
    But,
Remember Christians, Emigrants, Negroes
    deserve
A place upon this Overland Emigrant
    California train
and
Independence in
America, too!

I am the happiest I can be in this moment to know
that Mister Beckwourth and Miss Wheatley have
helped me to write my poem! And now I come out
of my dream to hear Mister Beckwourth and Poppa
as they continue to talk.

"The man, Jason, speaks about your horseman-
ship," Mister Beckwourth says. Poppa smiles. "I'd be
obliged if you would take a look at my horse."

"Be mighty happy to," Poppa says, smiling as he
walks away from us.

I watch with worry as the two men go to where the horses are tied. As I study Poppa from behind, wearing his company frock coat, I realize he does not look like Poppa. He does not look like the Ezekiel who tended the wagons and horses and served the meals at Belle Hills Farm. He looks like a new kind of Ezekiel.

I give a worried look to Momma. *Will Poppa keep walking away from us?* I wonder.

"Poppa?" I call to him, and start after them. He turns to me and waves me back not to follow.

It has been the biggest of days. I try to keep my eyes open to greet him on his return to our campfire, but tired sleep finds me. I only hope Poppa is not walking away from us as some other people have.

The next morning I awake with a start. Poppa! Has he walked away to join the mountain men? I look around. The frontiersmen have gotten an early start and gone. I do not have to look far for Poppa. He is cleaning out the dirt and gritty sand that gathers in the tight places of the wheels and spreading grease on the axles. Poppa says nothing of the mountain men.

The next day our journey forward leads us above the Carson River Valley over hills and mountains. It stretches for miles ahead. Mister Walter points to the most beautiful mountain and calls it the snowcapped butte. "That's a sight to see," he says.

We cross the river twice during the day by easy, safe, shallow waters.

On we go for miles and miles. Mister Walter and Mister Cooper are sure we are within a week's travel of the Sacramento Valley. The feelings of the people of the camp have changed. We all are weary, but there is a feeling of ease, too. We know we are coming to the end of our journey. We camp that night in a fine place on the river.

It all happens so suddenly. First, there is music and singing. The night is calm. The stars shine brightly. But the happiness in the air does not seem to affect Mister Jason. He is in a quiet mood—almost brooding. He sits with his back toward us facing away from our campfire. Then he speaks. And when he speaks, there is a sharpness to his words. He aims them all at Poppa.

"Ezekiel!" he snaps. His words and the sound of them remind me of Mister Uncle's voice and the way he spoke to Poppa. "It is time to start putting our minds back into civilization. We have been in this wilderness long enough." He barely looks at Poppa as he walks past.

On this long road, and while he was back home in Virginia planning this journey, Mister Jason treated

Poppa more like his friend than someone who serves him—asking Poppa for his advice. Out in this wilderness the bond between Poppa and Mister Jason seemed to grow stronger. There was a smoothness about the way they talked with each other or made a decision about one thing or another.

Mister Jason sought Poppa's opinion on most things and seemed satisfied with his judgment. At Belle Hills it would never have been abided for Poppa to speak so easily to Mister Jason first.

Now Poppa stands still and says nothing. It is as if Mister Jason has not said a word to him. He has not turned his body to face him either. Poppa keeps his back to Mister Jason.

"Ezekiel, I have spoken to you!" Mister Jason demands. "Acknowledge that you have heard me."

Slowly Poppa faces Mister Jason. His breathing is calm and easy. Poppa's face is soft—there are no hard lines around his mouth. We are all waiting to hear Poppa's answer. He has been ordered to speak. But Mister Jason does not wait to hear Poppa.

"We have all had a grand adventure." He gestures his hands around him. "All, wouldn't you say?" Mister Jason speaks in a softer tone now.

"Yes, it has been that," Poppa chuckles. "It has been a mighty, mighty adventure." Mister Jason smiles at Poppa's friendliness. Then Poppa pauses for longer than seems normal in a conversation with someone of Mister Jason's station. I lean forward waiting to hear what Poppa will finally say.

"I have seen the elephant . . . ," Poppa says.

"Yes, yes, yes. We all have many times on this trail," Mister Jason says.

". . . and I cannot be fitted back down now," Poppa says as he works to put his words together in the right order.

"Yes," Poppa starts again. "I have seen the elephant and I do not plan to return to Virginia."

"What do you mean, you do not plan to return to Virginia?"

"I am a free man."

"What do you mean? Free."

"Your father, Mister Howard, freed me long before he died—long before he journeyed by sea, and we lost him." Poppa lowers his head. "Your father was a good man to me. He valued my work. He was a good man— good to my family. He was a fair man as I am sure you aim to be, and as he would want you to be. In many ways he showed me and my family a great kindness. When he gave me freedom papers, he asked me to promise to stay on and tend the horses as I have. And I agreed. I agreed because of my wife and my newborn daughter." He points his head toward me. "Your mother has done right by us. She knows these things as I do.

"Before your father died, we spoke often together about working to pay for their freedom. He gave me my freedom papers long ago. I could have gone, but I stayed for them and for my promise to your father.

"I feel I have done my duty to your father—to your family and to you. Within a week or less, we will be brought to the gold fields. I will help you mine for gold, if you like, but the mountain man guide, Mister Beckwourth, said some mines do not welcome my kind there. I do not know how this will go. I know you will find your friend Richard Smith soon.

"As I always have, I will do my best toward you. But having seen *this* elephant, I know I will not return to Virginia. I cannot. I feel suited to these wide-open spaces. We will make our home in this new place, in this new land."

"I will not hear of this, this betrayal," Mister Jason starts. "I counted on you, and now you betray me. Do not think you can do this. The law will be on my side. You are owed to a cousin in Missouri!" Then, he turns and quietly begins to walk away from our campfire. But I run after him.

"Mister Jason," I call. "Please, wait," I plead as I follow him. "I *must* speak with you, Jason," I say. I hesitate because I know for the moment, I have forgotten myself. "It is about what I read in Mistress's letter.

What your mother wrote to me—what she said to me in her letter.

"I did not know what to do about it until now," I begin telling him. "I did not know those things about your poppa and my poppa. I did not know the two of them had an understanding. And I did not know Poppa would say those things. But he is right. I think you know he is right. Mistress Barnett, your mother, has given me my freedom papers, too."

"What does being right have to do—"

"Everything. Remember?" I hesitate. "Remember in the story of Jason and the Argonauts? Remember Mistress read to us? At the end of each of the stories your mother would have us *discuss*—talk about what we had just read—to discover the meaning inside the story.

"It was always the best part of everything to talk about what we read in the stories. It made me learn how to think about myself. I am grateful to your mother for the gifts she gave me."

"Yes, I remember . . . we had to decide upon a moral, a lesson—what the story was teaching us."

"Remember what you said to be the moral of Jason and the Argonauts?"

Mister Jason looks at me. For a moment he has no words. I am feeling afraid.

"I remember," he says. I look him in his eyes.

"Mistress Elizabeth helped us to understand the moral of the story. We all said we thought it was about greed and jealousy. The uncle's greed and jealousy caused so many bad things to happen. It was about greed. And she asked us what we thought of it.

"And you, being the quickest and the eldest, gave the best answer for us that day. Do you remember what you said?" I ask him.

"I remember," he says. "Being greedy never benefits anyone."

"I remember that," I say, and smile.

"Mistress worried and was distressed about this talk of gold and riches. Once she had told me how the search and desire for such things can change a person. It was something she did not want—not for you, her beloved firstborn. Of all children, she loved you first. You know this. She said this to you many times before," I say, surprised that the words that I have been holding on to in my head are now spilling out.

"I think you know your mother better than I. But this is what she said to me."

We stand under the stars as if we are strangers meeting for the very first time. As if whatever tie that holds us is being pulled tight enough to break. I think

we are strangers meeting for the first time. We all have become different people, new people. Here we have crossed these plains in this wilderness, and I am reminded of Mister Cooper's words:

"This journey will change you. Whoever you are and whatever you started out to be at the beginning of this journey, these plains we are about to cross will change you. And that is good. You will come out of this more than who you know yourself to be if you allow it. The road up ahead will require that and more of you."

It is true, we all have become someone more than we ever knew ourselves to be.

Three days later, we enter a spacious valley that is rich with soil. Instead of crossing the river, we stay close under the mountainside along the bank. We come to a place where wild cherry and plum bushes grow. We stop to add them for our evening meal. It is here in this place the world for me opens wider than the wilderness we've crossed.

A man rides up to our train on horseback. He stops and calls to us.

"You are only miles from the diggings."

Cheers and laughter and happiness rise up along our train.

"Our journey is good as done!" someone calls out.

There are whoops and yells and peals of laughter. Music plays.

"Oh! Susannah! Oh, don't you cry for me.
I'm bound for Cal-I forn-y
with my banjo on my knee."

Momma laughs as she looks around at us.

"We certainly look like a ragtag group," she says. It is true of the whole company. Many of our belongings are left back on the road. The clothes we are wearing are all we have left, and they have barely held up.

"Some of us are barefoot," she says. And she looks down at her worn boots and she laughs loudly.

"When I get off this trail," she continues, "it will be a long time before I eat another piece of bacon or salt pork. No more pulling and hauling wagons or hauling any kind of a load—for a while. But I am just glad we made it this far safely."

"We are no longer emigrants!" someone says. "Now we are all miners—miners for gold!"

I think on this idea of gold—something precious—a treasure of riches—something you find in the ground. For me and my family our gold is each other and our freedom.

On this road, there is no telling when and where you may see the elephant. And even now, standing in this beautiful valley, I believe the elephant might be my own poppa, standing before my eyes. Poppa stretches taller with his hands hitched at his waist. When he speaks, he stretches his arms out wide to draw Momma and me near. He says the truest words that can ever be heard.

"No," Poppa says. "We are not emigrants. We are nothing else but free. We. My family. Free! And our journey starts now!"

Epilogue

My dearest ~~Clementine~~ Hope,

I hope this letter finds you well. There are still many stories in the newspaper of travelers to California and the gold fields. I am glad I have not read of you. That tells me you are all safe.

I do not know where you will be when you read this note. And I do not think you will return to me here and to Belle Hills Farm. Whether Jason finds his golden fleece or not is not the reason I am saying this.

This letter gives you ownership of yourself. You are free.

Elizabeth Barnett

AUTHOR'S NOTE

History and our understanding of it evolve as we evolve. To me, it is like a giant puzzle being put together in real time, adding to the picture we have of a past recorded and known event. As time goes on, we realize layers are uncovered that reveal a deeper and broader viewpoint. Above all else, I think our grasp of history is the tip of the iceberg.

Stories of the west and the wilds of it fascinated me as a child. That fascination helped me to write *Thunder Rose*. Then, while compiling research for writing *Eliza's Freedom Road*, I came across a story of an enslaved person who was forced to accompany the slave owner to the gold fields of California to mine for gold. The man, with the aid of friendly White neighbors, was able to "free" himself by "hiding out" and then "disappearing." The idea fascinated and stuck with me. California did not receive statehood until 1850. And though it was anti-slavery, it was not anti-racist. In many instances, Blacks were not welcome in the mines.

For *Eliza*, the research material was limitless and boundless. For this journey west, it was quite another story. Gratefully, I was able to access the vast database of primary sources, diaries, and firsthand accounts of the way west from our most valuable resource, the Library of Congress. My personal connection to all of this is the idea of liberty and freedom—the founding bedrock of this nation. How in the midst of all the entanglements does one make oneself free? In a country whose existence is rooted in the idea of freedom, emancipation, and liberty, it is a curious question as to how to answer these things.

At the time when the United States was asserting and encouraging expansion of its western borders for exploration and settlements, a dynamic and life-changing event occurred. Gold was found. This created a caravan adventure for the sensibilities of the United States—the American spirit. The idea of westward expansion brought with it a sense of courage and defiance. Those who were able to travel had a streak of adventure and willingness to let go of what was known and start over with the new. As civilization gave way to the wilderness, each individual was confronted with the self, others, nature, and the universe. It was the mysterious circumstances that drove these adventurers to search for something greater and more.

When we think about the westward movement, very seldom do we think about the perspective of Indigenous people or enslaved people, as if they are not considered to have taken part in this particular time in history. *Hope's Path to Glory* is an attempt to expand the reader's understanding of this historical period. Hope, our faithful narrator, becomes a practiced observer of life as it changes for her and her family on their complex journey west and to freedom.

HISTORICAL BACKGROUND NOTE

When President Thomas Jefferson commissioned the Lewis and Clark expedition with the Corps of Discovery in 1803, it accomplished many things, but three in particular. Merriweather Lewis and William Clark were able to bring back notes and journals that mapped uncharted lands, rivers, and mountains. There were details about Native Americans and scientific information about the animals and plants of the region. There was also the dream—the magical and mystical stories about the west. It added to and sparked the imagination and spirit of adventure of the flourishing nation.

In 1840 Democratic presidential candidate James K. Polk ran on a platform of expanding the territory of the United States westward. In 1845 journalist John L. O'Sullivan coined the phrase "manifest destiny" to express the US thirst for expansion. This philosophy drove the nineteenth-century idea of westward movement in the United States.

Then something unexpected occurred that propelled the idea even further. In 1848 carpenter James W. Marshall discovered gold at Sutter's Mill at the South Fork of the American River. With the discovery of gold confirmed, this set up the greatest movement of voluntary migration in United States history. Southern farmers saw this as an opportunity to enhance their profits or finance their failing farms.

Some were known to travel to California with their enslaved workers to have them mine for the gold they sought. But how did all of this impact the individual—an individual family?

In the meantime, under the banner of the ideas brought forth in the Constitution of the United States, large populations of people from various nations and cultures were determining how to exist side by side.

Of special note—license has been taken with the story for historical impact. For example, it would have been unlikely that Hope would have known about Phillis Wheatley's poem at the time that this story was to take place.

Regarding the different Native tribes the emigrants encountered on the Overland Trail: at one time, Native tribes populated the entirety of the North American continent. As Europeans came to make this "new world" their home, the land we now know as the United States, a great shift and movement of Native people began. After the 1830 Indian Removal Act became law, those different nations of people were relocated to make way for westward expansion. During the passing years, tribes may have been forced to relocate again, or they may have taken it upon themselves to do so on their own. All of these shifts made it difficult to pinpoint where groups were at times on the trail. I painstakingly did the best I could with the resources I had at the time to represent this correctly.

TIME LINE

1769

The Spanish arrive in California. The population consists mostly of Californios (people of Spanish and Mexican descent), foreigners from America, and Native Americans.

1803

The Louisiana Purchase is made, through which the United States acquires the imperial rights to the land of the western half of the Mississippi River Basin from France. Napoleon Bonaparte needs the money for the Great French War. The deal grants the United States the sole authority to obtain the land from its indigenous inhabitants, either by contract or conquest. President Thomas Jefferson wants the land for future protection, expansion, prosperity, and the mystery of unknown lands.

MAY 14, 1804–SEPTEMBER 23, 1806

President Jefferson commissions Merriweather Lewis and William Clark to head the Corps of Discovery, a group of forty men, including the enslaved servant known as York, and go from St. Louis to the Pacific Ocean for a nearly eight-thousand-mile round-trip expedition. On the Corps's return in September 1806, the city of St. Louis becomes known by mountain men, adventurers, and settlers who followed as the "Gateway to the West."

1811–1860
The Oregon Trail, stretching for about two thousand miles, is laid by fur traders and trappers, and is only passable on foot or horseback. By 1836, the first migrant wagon train is organized in Independence, Missouri.

JULY 27, 1817
The first steamboat arrives in St. Louis.

MAY 28, 1830
Legislation called the Indian Removal Act is signed into law by President Andrew Jackson, authorizing land grants west of the Mississippi in exchange for lands within existing state borders. Some tribes go peacefully, but many resist the relocation policy. During the fall and winter of 1838 and 1839, the Cherokee are forcibly moved west by the United States government. Approximately four thousand Cherokee die on this forced march, which later became known as the Trail of Tears.

1839
John Sutter, a Swiss citizen, comes to California fleeing bankruptcy and financial failures, and leaving behind his wife and children in Switzerland. Sutter

persuades the Mexican governor to grant him lands on the Sacramento River.

1840

A steady and increasing fascination with California continues to grow. Parades of American emigrants from the East Coast of the United States come by way of an overland crossing rather than by sea aboard merchant ships.

1841

Sutter builds Sutter's Fort to set up frontier businesses for traders, trappers, and immigrants. He does not trade fairly with Native people.

JULY 1845–AUGUST 1845

The term "manifest destiny" is coined by journalist John L. O'Sullivan, who wrote in favor of US expansion based on the idea that the United States is destined by God to spread democracy across the continent.

1845

Lansford W. Hastings publishes *The Emigrants' Guide to Oregon and California*, the first major guidebook of its kind depicting the way west.

DECEMBER 2, 1845

President James K. Polk's first State of the Union

address promises the idea that the United States should stretch "from sea to shining sea."

April 14, 1846

The families of brothers George and Jacob Donner and local businessman James Reed leave Springfield, Illinois. Reaching Independence, Missouri, they become part of a main wagon train heading west to California. Using *The Emigrants' Guide to Oregon and California*, the group takes a shortcut recommended by Hastings, known now as the Hastings Cutoff. The shortcut proves disastrous, resulting in their having to survive the winter lost and unprepared in the Sierra Nevada Mountains and resorting to cannibalism.

May 12, 1846

President Polk requests that Congress declare war on Mexico because of land and border disputes.

January 24, 1848

While building a water-powered sawmill, a carpenter and mechanic from New Jersey named James W. Marshall finds flakes of gold in a streambed of the American River. Miwok, Maidu, and Nisenan tribes help Marshall dig a millrace at Sutter's Mill. The influx of miners brings disease that kills thousands of Native people.

FEBRUARY 28, 1848

The Mexican-American War ends. The area of California operates under military rule of the United States.

MARCH 15, 1848

A San Francisco newspaper publishes reports of the discovery of gold.

MAY 12, 1848

A merchant runs up and down the streets of San Francisco, raising a bottle full of golden crystals and shouting, "Gold, gold, gold from the American River!" Many of the men in San Francisco leave the city in search of gold.

AUGUST 19, 1848

The *New York Herald* newspaper reports that gold is found in California.

NOVEMBER 1948

The first shipments of gold leave San Francisco, totaling $500,000.

DECEMBER 5, 1848

President Polk confirms to the young nation that gold has indeed been found in California. This leads many people to begin the migration west in hopes of finding gold.

1849

People come to California from around the world to get rich. They become known as the "forty-niners."

1850

California enters the union, becoming the thirty-first state, but the question of slavery has not been decided. Another shipment of gold leaves San Francisco in the amount of $1.5 million. Gold runs out!

1852

Sutter is bankrupt.

1855

The Gold Rush ends.

1863

On March 26, 1863, during the Civil War, the western section of Virginia ratifies a revised state constitution to include the gradual emancipation of slaves (Virginia gained statehood in 1788, stretching as far the Mississippi River). On June 20, 1863, President Lincoln proclaims West Virginia officially a state.

1865

Sutter's home is destroyed by arson. He moves to Pennsylvania.

SOURCE LIST

CHAPTER ONE
A BROKEN HOME

The Daily Union (Washington, DC). January 27, 1849. Library of Congress, Washington, DC. https://www.loc.gov/resource /sn82003410/1849-01-27/ed-1/?sp=3&st=image.

Frederick Douglass Papers at the Library of Congress. Library of Congress, Washington, DC. https://www.loc.gov/collections /frederick-douglass-papers/about-this-collection.

A Guide to the History of Slavery in Maryland. The Maryland State Archives, Annapolis Maryland, and the University of Maryland College Park, Maryland. 2007. https://msa.maryland .gov/msa/intromsa/pdf/slavery_pamphlet.pdf.

National Park Service. "Frederick Douglass." US Department of the Interior. Last updated August 3, 2022. https://www.nps .gov/frdo/learn/historyculture/frederickdouglass.htm.

"Phillis Wheatley's Poem on Tyranny and Slavery, 1772." The Gilder Lehrman Institute of American History. https://www .gilderlehrman.org/sites/default/files/inline-pdfs/06154_FPS_0.pdf.

Sorensen, Leni. "Enslaved House Servants." In *Encyclopedia Virginia.* Virginia Humanities. January 20, 2022. https:// encyclopediavirginia.org/entries/enslaved-house-servants.

Wheatley, Phillis. "On Being Brought from Africa to America." Poetry Foundation. https://www.poetryfoundation.org /poems/45465/on-being-brought-from-africa-to-america.

CHAPTER TWO
TRAVELING TO THE END OF THE WORLD

The Daily Union (Washington, DC). January 27, 1849. Library of Congress, Washington, DC. https://www.loc.gov/resource /sn82003410/1849-01-27/ed-1/?sp=3&st=image.

"Distressing News." *California Star* (San Francisco), February 13, 1847. The Museum of the City of San Francisco. http://www .sfmuseum.org/hist6/donner.html.

Disturnell, John. *Mapa de los Estados Unidos de Mejico.* 1847. US National Archives. https://www.archives.gov/files/publications /prologue/2005/summer/images/mexico-disturnell-l.jpg.

Hastings, Lansford W. *The Emigrants' Guide to Oregon and California.* 1845.

"James K. Polk." From *The Presidents of the United States of America* by Frank Freidel and Hugh Sidey. White House Historical Association. 2006. https://www.whitehouse.gov /about-the-white-house/presidents/james-k-polk.

Marcy, Randolph B. *The Prairie Traveler.* Commissioned by authority of the War Department. (New York: Harper & Brothers, 1859).

O'Sullivan, John. "Annexation." *United States Magazine and Democratic Review* 17, no. 1 (July–August 1845): 5–6, 9–10. https://pdcrodas.webs.ull.es/anglo/OSullivanAnnexation.pdf.

CHAPTER THREE
LEAVING HOME

Edward Weber & Co. *Map Showing the Connection of the Baltimore and Ohio Railroad with Other Railroads Executed or In Progress throughout the United States.* 184?. Library of Congress, Washington, DC. https://www.loc.gov/item/gm 70002855.

"Food Along the Overland Trail." History Nebraska. https://history.nebraska.gov/publications/food-along-overland-trail.

Gilbert, David T. "Route of Meriwether Lewis from Harpers Ferry, Va. to Pittsburgh, Pa. July 8–July 15, 1803." National Park Service. US Department of the Interior. September 28, 2015. https://www.nps.gov/hafe/learn/historyculture/route-from-harpers-ferry-va-to-pittsburgh-pa.htm.

Schuchman, William, and the Central Ohio Railroad Company. *Map of Central Ohio Connecting Lines.* 1850. Library of Congress, Washington, DC. https://www.loc.gov/resource/g3711p.rr00362 0/?r=-0.001,-0.014,0.5,0.258,0.

CHAPTER FOUR
BEGINNING THE TRAIL TO THE NEW WORLD

Burns, C. R., et al. *The Commonwealth of Missouri, a Centennial Record.* 1877. Library of Congress, Washington, DC. https://www.loc.gov/resource/gdcmassbookdig.commonwealthofmi01 barn/?sp=1&st=slideshow#slide-66.

Child, Andrew. *Overland Route to California*. (Los Angeles: N. A. Kovach, 1946). https://babel.hathitrust.org/cgi/pt?id=uva .x000610311&view=1up&seq=10.

Cohen, Olly. "Medicinal Plants, Herbs, and Trees of Missouri." Washington University in St. Louis. December 30, 2019. https://sites.wustl.edu/monh/medicinal-plants-herbs-and-trees -of-missouri.

"Disrupting the Natives." Oregon-California Trails Association. https://octa-trails.org/articles/disrupting-the-natives.

Fitzgerald, Colin. "African American Slave Medicine of the 19th Century." Bridgewater State University. *Undergraduate Review*, 12 (2016): 44–50. https://vc.bridgew.edu/cgi/viewcontent.cgi?art icle=1376&context=undergrad_rev.

Fowke, Gerard, and the Archaeological Institute of America. *Antiquities of Central and Southeastern Missouri*. 1910. Library of Congress, Washington, DC. https://www.loc.gov/resource /gdcmassbookdig.antiquitiesofcenoofowk/?st=gallery.

Indian Removal Act: Primary Documents in American History. Library of Congress, Washington, DC. https://guides.loc.gov /indian-removal-act.

National Park Service. "The Osage." US Department of the Interior. Last updated May 25, 2022. https://www.nps.gov/fosc /learn/historyculture/osage.htm.

Von Hoffmann, Albert. *All about Saint Louis*. c. 1923. Library of Congress, Washington, DC. https://www.loc.gov/resource /gdcmassbookdig.vonhoffmannsallaoovonh/?sp=15.

Chapter Five
Traveling with Wagons, Mules, Oxen, Dogs, and Men

National Park Service. *California Trail*. US Department of the Interior. https://www.nps.gov/cali/planyourvisit/upload/CALImap1-web.pdf.

National Park Service. "Missouri." US Department of the Interior. Last updated January 6, 2022. https://www.nps.gov/cali/planyourvisit/missouri.htm.

National Park Service. "Fort Kearny State Historical Park." US Department of the Interior. Last updated December 10, 2021. https://www.nps.gov/places/000/fort-kearny-state-historical-park.htm.

National Park Service. "Wayne City (Upper Independence) Landing." US Department of the Interior. Last updated November 29, 2021. https://www.nps.gov/places/000/wayne-city-upper-independence-landing.htm.

Chapter Six
New Ways of Cooking and Eating

California Trail Interpretive Center. "Fort Laramie." Southern Nevada Conservancy. https://www.californiatrailcenter.org/fort-laramie.

National Park Service. *California Trail*. US Department of the Interior. https://www.nps.gov/cali/planyourvisit/upload/CALImap1-web.pdf.

National Park Service. "Chimney Rock." US Department of the Interior. Last updated August 31, 2022. https://www.nps.gov /scbl/learn/historyculture/chimney-rock.htm.

National Park Service. "Chimney Rock National Historic Site." US Department of the Interior. Last updated February 21, 2020. https://www.nps.gov/cali/planyourvisit/chimney-rock.htm.

National Park Service. "Courthouse and Jail Rocks." US Department of the Interior. Last updated October 8, 2022. https://www.nps.gov/places/000/courthouse-and-jail-rocks.htm.

National Park Service. "Crossroads of a Nation Moving West." US Department of the Interior. Last updated September 24, 2022. https://www.nps.gov/fola/index.htm.

National Park Service. "A Landmark for Many Peoples." US Department of the Interior. Last updated September 20, 2022. https://www.nps.gov/scbl/index.htm.

National Park Service. *Scotts Bluff: Military & Supply Forts on the Oregon Trail*. US Department of the Interior. http://npshistory .com/brochures/scbl/forts-on-the-oregon-trail.pdf.

National Park Service. *Scotts Bluff: Traveling the Emigrant Trails*. US Department of the Interior. http://npshistory.com /brochures/scbl/traveling-the-emigrant-trails.pdf.

CHAPTER SEVEN
MUCH BEAUTY ALONG THE TRAIL

California Trail Interpretive Center. "The Sweetwater River." Southern Nevada Conservancy. https://www.californiatrail center.org/the-sweetwater-river.

"Independence Rock Historic Site." Wyoming State Parks, Historic Sites, & Trails. https://wyoparks.wyo.gov/index.php /places-to-go/independence-rock.

National Park Service. *California Trail*. US Department of the Interior. https://www.nps.gov/cali/planyourvisit/upload /CALImap1-web.pdf.

National Park Service. "Devil's Gate." US Department of the Interior. Last updated February 12, 2019. https://www.nps.gov /cali/planyourvisit/devils-gate.htm.

National Park Service. "Independence Rock." US Department of the Interior. Last updated February 12, 2019. https://www .nps.gov/cali/planyourvisit/independence-rock.htm.

National Park Service. "South Pass." US Department of the Interior. Last updated February 12, 2019. https://www.nps.gov /cali/planyourvisit/south-pass.htm.

Chapter Eight
The Long, Hard Road

National Park Service. *California Trail*. US Department of the Interior. https://www.nps.gov/cali/planyourvisit/upload/CALImap1-web.pdf.

National Park Service. "Soda Springs, Glen Aulin, Waterwheel Falls Trailhead." US Department of the Interior. Last updated April 16, 2021. https://www.nps.gov/places/000/soda-springs-glen-aulin-waterwheel-falls-trailhead.htm.

Chapter Nine
Sierra Nevada Mountains—
The Donner Party

"California Trail." Trails West. https://emigranttrailswest.org/virtual-tour/california-trail.

National Park Service. *California Trail*. US Department of the Interior. https://www.nps.gov/cali/planyourvisit/upload/CALImap1-web.pdf.

Chapter Ten
Meeting Someone Familiar and New—
Frontiersman Jim Beckwourth

An Act Respecting Slaves, Free Negroes, and Mulattoes. 1847. Missouri Secretary of State's Office. https://www.sos.mo.gov/CMSImages/MDH/AnActRespectingSlaves,1847.pdf.

African Americans: Gold Rush Era to 1900. University of California. 2005. https://calisphere.org/exhibitions/47/african -americans-gold-rush.

"Black Miners Bar, Folsom Lake State Recreation Area." California Department of Parks and Recreation. https://www .parks.ca.gov/?page_id=27866.

Bonner, T. D. *The Life and Adventures of James P. Beckwourth, Mountaineer, Scout, Pioneer, and Chief of the Crow Nation of Indians: Written from His Own Dictation.* (New York: Harper & Brothers, 1856).

California Trail Interpretive Center. "Landmarks along the California Trail." Southern Nevada Conservancy. https://www .californiatrailcenter.org/landmarks-along-the-california-trail.

Delano, Alphonso. *Life on the Plains and among the Diggings; Being Scenes and Adventures of an Overland Journey to California.* (New York: Miller, Orton & Co., 1857). https://tile.loc.gov /storage-services//service/gdc/calbk/171.pdf.

"Distressing News." *California Star* (San Francisco), February 13, 1847. The Museum of the City of San Francisco. http://www .sfmuseum.org/hist6/donner.html.

"The Forty Niners." Library of Congress, Washington, DC. https://www.loc.gov/collections/california-first-person -narratives/articles-and-essays/early-california-history/forty -niners.

Houghton, Elizabeth P. Donner. *The Expedition of the Donner Party and Its Tragic Fate.* (Chicago: A. C. McClurg & Co., 1911). https://tile.loc.gov/storage-services//service/gdc/calbk/187.pdf.

Journals and Drawings of J. Goldsborough Bruff, 1849–1853. The Huntington Library, Art Museum and Botanical Gardens. https://hdl.huntington.org/digital/collection/p15150coll7/search /searchterm/Bruff%2C%20Joseph%20Goldsborough%2C%20 1804-1889%2C%20artist./field/creato/mode/exact/conn/and.

National Park Service. *California Trail*. US Department of the Interior. https://www.nps.gov/cali/planyourvisit/upload /CALImap1-web.pdf.

National Park Service. "Death and Danger on the Emigrant Trails." US Department of the Interior. Last updated December 29, 2020. https://www.nps.gov/articles/000/death-on-trails.htm.

National Park Service. "Gold Fever!" US Department of the Interior. Last updated January 5, 2021. https://www.nps.gov /cali/index.htm.

National Park Service. "Maps." US Department of the Interior. Last updated August 31, 2021. https://www.nps.gov/cali /planyourvisit/maps.htm.

Read, Georgia Willis, and Ruth Gaines, eds. *Gold Rush: The Journals, Drawings, and Other Papers of J. Goldsborough Bruff, Captain, Washington City and California Mining Association, April 2, 1849–July 20, 1851.* (New York: Columbia University Press, 1944).

Sherman, Gen. William T. *Recollections of California 1846–1861.* (Berkeley, California: The Gillick Press, 1945). https://tile.loc .gov/storage-services//service/gdc/calbk/085.pdf.

Sutter, John Augustus, and Douglas S. Watson. *The Diary of Johann August Sutter.* (San Francisco: The Grabhorn Press, 1932).

"Traveling on the Overland Trails 1843–1860." Library of
Congress, Washington, DC. https://www.loc.gov/classroom
-materials/united-states-history-primary-source-timeline
/national-expansion-and-reform-1815-1880/traveling-on-the
-overland-trails-1843-1860.

"West in a Wagon Train: Three Questions." Oregon-California
Trails Association. January 2018. https://octa-trails.org/wp
-content/uploads/2018/01/524_West-in-a-Wagon-Train.pdf.

Wrenn, Sara B., and Jean C. Slauson. *Early Pioneer Life*.
January 1939. Library of Congress, Washington DC.
https://www.loc.gov/resource/wpalh2.29091524/?sp=18&st=text.

ACKNOWLEDGMENTS

Being a lifelong reader and writer, I am always interested to discover how things happen in the world, especially how books come together to arrive on our shelves. It is close to a miracle, and magical besides, when it occurs.

This book could not have been without the support and encouragement of so many dear loved ones, friends, and loyal allies, as well as our country's enduring cultural institutions. Of special note was having access to our shared American heritage through the rich and diverse cultural resources housed in the Library of Congress, as well as the National Park Service. The librarians and park rangers who represent our institutions were most valuable in helping me locate information, no matter how obscure. Kathy Conway at the Oregon-California Trails Association, Nikia Parker of the Osage Nation, and Lee Kreutzer of the Utah National Trails Office were especially helpful. The use of technology to access digital resources at the library placed historical texts at my fingertips.

When I started this book journey, I had no idea the vast undertaking it would turn out to be. Like the journey, I am changed by it. This was indeed a trek through a wilderness trail. I have deep appreciation for all who took this journey with me. Special thanks, first and foremost, to Paula Wiseman, my most wise and treasured editor, whose belief in my vision helped to sustain me. I cherish my literary adventure with her. To the copy editors and their attention to detail. To Nancy Gallt, my beloved agent, who has held my hand steadfastly through these years and whose advice and support I could not do without. And to Marietta Zacker, who keeps the agency's support seamless.

To Pat Cummings, a wonderful friend, colleague, and untiring supporter for so many of us committed to excellent literature for children. To my dear friend Sharon Kalin, who listens deeply and hears wisely.

To my sister, Genice Suggs, the finest cheerleader a sister can ever have. To my brother, Eugene Nolen, and his wife, Joan, who welcomed me each time I needed to camp out in their California home when I visited the area where I studied. To my dear children, Matthew Harold and Jessica Harold, whose love, support, and devotion I could not live without. It is that kind of love and belief in me that causes me to remember the goodness in the world and the possibility of all things.

ABOUT THE AUTHOR

Jerdine Nolen is the beloved author of many award-winning books, including *Big Jabe*; *Thunder Rose*, a Coretta Scott King Illustrator Honor Book; and *Hewitt Anderson's Great Big Life*, a Bank Street Best Book of the Year, all illustrated by Kadir Nelson. She is also the author of *Eliza's Freedom Road*, illustrated by Shadra Strickland, which was an ALA/YALSA Best Fiction Nominee for Young Adults; *Raising Dragons*, illustrated by Elise Primavera, which received the Christopher Award; and *Harvey Potter's Balloon Farm*, illustrated by Mark Buehner, which was made into the movie *Balloon Farm*. Her other books include *Calico Girl*, a *Kirkus Reviews* Best Book of the Year, and *Irene's Wish*, illustrated by A.G. Ford, which *Kirkus Reviews* called "delightful and memorable" in a starred review. Ms. Nolen lives in Maryland.